www.TakeOneWithYou.com

# TAKE ONE WITH YOU

## OAK ANDERSON

Mom and Dad

Thank you for your guidance and an incredible life. I love you.

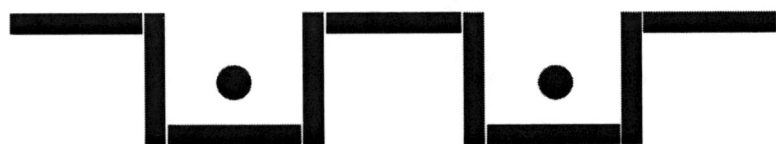

*"Death may be the greatest of all human blessings."*

-Socrates

*"It's better to burn out than fade away."*

-Kurt Cobain

*"We get what we deserve."*

- Melissa "clairebear" Williamson

***Take One With You (Sarah's Song) Towy Kings***
***Farmerland Music, LLC***

Gunshots after midnight, winter's on the way
You'll never see me comin', you'll never know my name

Let's try a poison cocktail, or blades will do just fine
We'll make it final, baby, just as long as you'll be mine

Be my Towy, baby
Breathe your last with me
Go with me, sweet Towy
Across a bloody sea

Accidents will happen and darkness will descend
It's never what you start off with that lasts until the end

The world's a better place because of what you take away
It's never what you think that makes you want to leave or stay

You'll never see me coming
You'll never change my mind
I'll take one with me, baby
Then take you one last time

Be my Towy, Charlie
Breathe your last with me
Be my friend, sweet Charlie
Across my bloody sea

They'll never see us coming
They'll never change our mind
Let's take one with us, baby
Then take me one last time

Be my Towy, baby
Breathe your last with me
Be my savior, baby
Across our bloody sea

Be my Towy, baby
Across our bloody sea

# Chapter One

"Take one if you want."

Max turned his attention from the sad, fading pictures over his soon-to-be-ex-cellie's bunk and glared at the pathetic piece of shit who'd pasted them there.

"Fuck you, faggot," he said with disgust, completely comfortable with the irony that he had systematically sodomized his weaker cellmate for most of his eighteen-month sentence. Max pled down to assault after the chick he'd viciously raped and beaten ended up with brain damage and couldn't remember dick. Time served on the reduced charge was the easiest time he'd ever done. Traumatic brain injury was definitely the way to go.

That and Rohypnol.

"You think I wanna keep looking at those ugly sluts a yours?"

Max would have given the smaller man a beat down just for the hell of it if he wasn't being released that very afternoon. *Not worth fucking that up for this shithead. Dumbass is doing life on the installment plan.*

Max pulled out his own photo, from a sweet blonde honey in daisy dukes who called herself Missy and promised to be waiting outside that very day. He wasn't sure how she'd found him since he didn't post those dumbass personal ads in *Horny Inmates Digest* or whatever fucking rag his cellie used, but if she didn't look like the picture, Missy was gonna get fucked up that very night. She'd get fucked up, anyway, of course, but if she was ugly he'd make it hurt a little extra. Max smiled. He couldn't decide which he preferred.

"Shit, she's fine," his cellmate said, leering over the photo.

Max quickly yanked it back before the asshole could grub it up. He felt like he should slap the shit out of him for good measure, but there was also an absurd pride in the fact that his paper doll was so much better looking than any of the loser bitches who lined his cellie's spank wall.

"Goddamn right she is," Max answered, and pocketed the picture.

"Let's go, Maxie."

He turned to see Leadhead, a smirking guard who'd brought a whole team with him just to escort Max downstairs where he'd process out.

"You must think I'm a real dangerous man," he jeered.

"You want we should come back after you book a whammer?" Leadhead asked, causing the other guards to bust up laughing at the thought of Big Max actually blowing his smaller cellmate.

"Fuck you," Max answered, but he had to chuckle at that one. *As if.*

***

He had to squint to see her as he walked out of the prison, but even with the blazing sun setting behind her, Max could tell by the silhouette that Missy was every bit as curvy in person as she was in the photograph.

He grinned and strode across the hot pavement where she was leaning against what looked like a brand new crotch rocket, spit-shined and gleaming, a helmet hanging from each handgrip. The closer he got, the better he liked. Looked like a bottle job, *but who gives a shit if the fucking curtains don't match.*

Her shirt was small, her shorts were tight, and those boots were definitely made for walking. Real slow and sexy-like.

"Big Max," she said when he stopped a few feet away, still slightly amazed at his good fortune.

"In the flesh."

"Been waitin' for my Bandit," she said, and he smiled even more broadly.

*This chick is a little crazy. Or stupid. Either way, I like it.*

"You know the Motel 6 in Porterville?" she asked, her lips wet and sultry.

Max nodded. He didn't, but he'd find it.

"Take me there."

Max leaned in, but she stuck a helmet in his gut, put the other one on, and motioned towards the bike.

"What'cha waitin' for, big man?"

Max grinned and put on the helmet, mounting the bike in a single, fluid motion. He'd caught a wild one, that was for damn sure. *Best play along till we get there.*

She climbed on behind him and wrapped her arms around his waist, hands clasped four inches north of heaven. Big Max was acutely aware of her soft body, its heat burning into his back. He didn't waste any time, starting the bike and roaring up the prison road towards Highway 99, grinning from ear-to-ear as he gunned past a slow-moving station wagon, reveling in the open road before him. He had no idea that would be his last memory for a very, very long time.

***

*"Melissa! Come inside, sweetie!"*

*Missy dropped the dented pail and ran towards the house, her dress shoes kicking up splotches of mud across her formerly pristine white dress. She banged into the house, the tattered screen door slamming open and closed behind her, leaving tracks across the worn beige carpeting that, like the rest of the furnishings, had seen much better days.*

*"Goddamnit!"*

*Her foster mother just stood there speechless as her husband cursed, his large, callused hands already moving to unbuckle his belt. The action seemed reflexive, almost like an involuntary motion over which he had no control, which was not far from the truth on most days, but especially when he drank.*

*His wife, a slight, drab woman who could blend into almost any background, stood aside and stared at the floor. She had learned long before not to get in between the man she married and any of her children, whether her own or the foster kids they took in for the money.*

*Bud was a violent man, but he did not discriminate.*

*"No, Daddy!"*

*Claire stepped in front of her younger sister, pleading eyes and resolute stance. She had managed to keep them together through several placements after the death of their parents, and often found herself in the role of protector. Melissa had behavioral problems, perfectly understandable in light of what she'd been through at such a young age, and several families had attempted to take in only the older, better-behaved girl. Claire, however, always seemed to know what to say and how to act to make sure that idea was never advanced and the girls stayed together.*

*Bud stopped in his tracks, but he finished taking off his belt. His wife turned away and gathered their two natural born children, silently moving them into the bedroom to wait out the storm.*

*Bud smiled grimly. He had to admire the pretty one's balls. "Have it your way, Princess."*

***

They were really flying now. Her hands were on his arms, lightly squeezing and scratching in an unspoken request for more speed, and Max eagerly complied. When he hit ninety, she reached down and squeezed something else, and he throttled up again. *This chick is fucking crazy,* he thought, *and I like it!*

Behind him, Missy's tears flowed like liquid fire, hissing in the wind as they burned off below her darkened faceguard.

***

*Claire stood before the judge in silence, watching intently as the old man looked through their voluminous case file. Melissa stood next to her, trying to conceal her fear. Usually just being near her older sister was enough to calm her nerves, but today was almost unbearable. Claire was barely seventeen, and even Missy understood that it was a lot to expect.*

*The judge finally looked up, somewhat bemused to see the two teenagers still standing as if there was a verdict to be read. He glanced at opposing counsel, who was idly sorting her other case files like a bored housewife examining swatches.*

*"You can sit down, you know," the judge said, not unkindly, but neither girl budged. The older one gave him a polite smile,*

*though, which he took as an understanding of some kind. He thought the younger girl looked ready to jump out of her skin, but every so often her sister would squeeze her hand and that seemed to quiet her younger sister's nerves. As the father of three girls, the judge remembered quite well what a task that could be at times.*

*He closed the file and considered the two young women.*

*Fourteen and seventeen, eyes as dark as their hair. Parents killed nine years ago by a drunk driver. What a life so far.*

*The judge looked at their court-appointed representative, who appeared to be texting beneath the table. He cleared his throat and got the social worker's attention, then spoke directly to the girls.*

*"I'm going to speak informally for a moment, is that all right?"*

*Claire answered in a clear, confident voice that was a bit too loud for the silent courtroom. "That's fine, Judge." She squeezed Melissa's hand and the younger girl nodded and may have said something he couldn't hear, or perhaps there was no sound at all.*

*"How many foster homes have you two been in, Claire?"*

*"Six."*

*"How many?"*

*"I don't count the Chadwicks," she said. "That was only a week."*

*The judge saw a faint smile almost lift the corners of the younger girl's mouth before falling back in line with the seriousness of her sister's tone.*

*"Do you really believe you can take care of yourself and your sister if I grant your motion?"*

*"Your Honor, the state doesn't believe Miss Williamson can care for herself, let alone her sister," the state's attorney interrupted, now fully roused from her sleepy swatches.*

*"Can, too!"*

*Everyone now looked at Melissa, whose vehemence was like a cannon shot across still waters.*

*This time it was the older girl who nearly smiled.*

*The judge looked at the state's attorney coldly and she promptly shut her mouth. The girls' caseworker, who a moment ago looked as if he was about to speak as well, now thought better of it and looked down at his legal pad to avoid a similar fate.*

*"I'm going to give you a chance, Claire," the judge said, turning his attention to the older girl, and the words were barely out of his mouth before the two sisters' four knees seemed to buckle at almost exactly the same time and they fell into each others' arms for support, as if an invisible bearing wall had collapsed between them.*

*The rest of the hearing was a blur, but both girls knew their lives were about to change forever. What they didn't know was that 'forever' would not last beyond a few short years.*

***

"Faster!" Missy screamed, and reached forward as far as she could, placing her hand over Max's and throttling up until they were going over a hundred miles an hour. She was hanging off the bike like some crazy bulldogger, and Max was once again both shocked and turned on by her recklessness.

Missy immediately ran her hand down his arm and then reached inside his shirt, caressing his prison-hardened chest for a moment before allowing her fingers to drift downward, and all other thoughts flew from his mind.

All Max knew was that this chick was going to take his rod in every hole and twice on Sunday.

"Goddamn, girl!" he screamed, and pushed the bike up to a hundred and ten. *Can't get to that motel fast enough!*

Missy ripped off her helmet with one hand and released it into the wind, the sound of it skittering across the grooved pavement behind them never reaching their ears. Her long blonde hair with her dark roots whipped around their heads like a frenzied, honey-colored tornado dancing around its blackened soul, and when she lifted his helmet off and let it go, Max was as horny as he had ever been in his life.

"I'm gonna fuck you good, you goddamn whore!" he screamed, but the sound of his voice, like everything else, was lost in the wind.

***

*Melissa threw open the door. She'd been up all night, frantic. Two police officers were standing there. She read the truth in their eyes, and burst into tears.*

***

For a moment everything stopped, as if the bike was moving so fast that time itself slowed. It seemed as if her consciousness had somehow released its bond to the physical world, and she was looking at its wonders not as a participant, but as an observer. She turned to the right and saw the landscape frozen in a kaleidoscope of color and form. Each sound was now a single, crystalline track not yet merged into a symphony of engine noise and wind and speed, and it was all perfectly clear and focused.

At that moment it almost seemed possible to just let go, both physically and emotionally. In an instant she could put it all behind her, erase everything that had been and everything that was to be. Nothing was set in stone. Nothing was inevitable. In her mind, Missy threw open her arms and tumbled backwards, floating in space, and the bitter cup passed from her lips and slowly faded outside her grasp into nothingness.

Was that how it felt for Claire? As her mind slowly gave way? As she finally buckled after so many years of relentless pressure and gave in to the world that had done nothing but crush her spirit? Or did it better describe her final thoughts as she laid tracks up her arms in that cheap motel, finally clear on her own final solution?

Her eyes found his in the side mirror. The eyes of the man who ruined everything. It wasn't the world. It was him. Missy looked into the eyes of the man who was responsible for Claire's death, and reality flooded back like a cold slap in the face.

"Almost there, baby!" he yelled, and it was then that he saw her eyes, really saw them for the first time in two years. And Big Max knew that he'd fucked up. He'd been blinded by the hair and the tits and the ass and the attitude, and he'd never really looked into those eyes. It was then that he saw her, really saw her, and knew things weren't going to go as he'd planned.

***

*Claire was never the same after the attack. The man who brutally raped and beat her also left her with devastating injuries, and she became a hollow shell, a mere shadow of her former self. For so long she had been her sister's keeper, but Melissa could not, in the end, take care of her older sister as she herself had been cared for.*

*Claire killed herself on the day the district attorney informed them that her attacker would be spending less than two years in prison. It was the final insult, and more than she could endure.*

*Melissa was tormented by guilt afterwards, and spent months in a deep depression from which she never really recovered. She was so distraught she rarely got out of bed, crying for hours every day and praying for the strength to end her life.*

*Claire had been everything to her since their parents died, and losing her left Melissa without a reason to go on. But she couldn't even rouse herself to end her suffering. It seemed a proper penance, or so she thought in more lucid moments, a fitting purgatory for failing her sister so badly.*

*On top of everything else, she would never measure up. Claire was the strong one, the pretty one, the best one. Missy had never wanted anything more than to be just like her Clairebear, but that dream had died along with her sister.*

*On the night she finally decided to end her life, a chance encounter online gave Melissa a reason to live for at least a little while longer. It was her epiphany, and she began to prepare for the end. Once she found the will to die, she knew she would do so with purpose, and that, at last, would give meaning to her life.*

***

Max wasn't going down without a fight.

At the moment he realized just who had actually been taken for a ride, his mind was already racing as to how he could stop the bike and beat the living shit out of the bitch on the back. She had stones, he had to give her that.

They were traveling at one hundred and thirteen miles an hour.

He let go of the throttle and slammed his fist down on her thigh as hard as he could. Melissa howled in pain and reached for the knife in her boot. He saw the glint in the mirror and not the weapon, but he managed to bring his elbow back hard, hitting her square in the nose, sending black, starry pain from her head to her toes and the knife clattering to the pavement behind them.

They were going a hundred and four.

She nearly fell off the back, but managed to get her arm around his neck, digging her fingernails into soft flesh, drawing blood. He screamed and tried to hit her again, but she dug the top of her head into the middle of his back.

They were moving at ninety-seven miles an hour.

As he flailed at her awkwardly, she reached underneath his arm and lunged for the throttle. He slapped her hand away.

"What the fuck are you doing?" he screamed, still not fully understanding. *Is the bitch crazy?*

She got hold of it on the second try. He elbowed the top of her head this time, but she held fast, and it was then that he made his fatal mistake, at ninety-two miles an hour.

Max hit her arm three times in succession, first striking her wrist, which caused the bike to throttle up, and then her forearm, fracturing her radius.

Missy screamed in pain, nearly blacking out, but she held onto the grip.

At that point, all Max had to do was to ease up on the throttle and onto the brake, guiding the bike to a stop. Missy had no strength at that point to either speed up the bike or yank the handlebar to the side, but Max had never been real smart about women, or anything else, for that matter, and he brought his fist down again.

With every last ounce of strength she possessed, Missy tightened her grip and held on, bracing for the blow. As he struck her arm, Max realized his mistake, but by then it was too late.

*Bitch doesn't want to kill me. She wants to kill us both.*

The front wheel yanked sharply to the right causing the bike to wobble violently and Big Max laid her down at one hundred and one miles an hour, the bike slamming them against the roadway and dragging them against the rough pavement, burning their flesh from the top and skinning it from below across seventy feet of asphalt.

Even his last instinct was a major fuck-up; had Max just let go and not tried to save himself, he might have survived in slightly better shape.

But Big Max was never very good at letting go of anything, one of the qualities, and there were many, that usually got him in trouble.

The bike finally hit an uneven spot in the pavement and flipped, mercifully extricating the two of them from its hellish embrace, and Missy was thrown off the road and into a ditch. Her back was broken, half her face was torn away, but when she closed her eyes all she saw was the smiling face of her sister.

Max opened his good eye and stared into the setting sun. For a moment he imagined he was lifting weights in the yard, listening to the chatter and enjoying the breeze, until he tried and failed to move his legs. He attempted to call out, but only swallowed blood. He managed to roll over, and saw his favorite tattoo lying on the road beside him.

*PUSSY*

He'd last seen that particular prison tat in the mirror, on the inside of his lower lip.

Suddenly Max wanted to scream, needed to, but could only gurgle and spit out coppery chunks of his own tongue. He fought the urge to touch his face, which he now felt sure was mostly gone. It was debatable whether he could raise his arm, anyway.

He remembered, but only for a moment, the blonde outside the prison gate, and after much effort, was able to look around for her. She'd disappeared like a whistle in the wind. Somehow he figured out that she must have been thrown clear of the road, and Big Max began to writhe his way to the edge of the road where he hoped he could watch her die. One of her boots stood up on its heel a few feet away, mocking his slow progression.

Missy, for her part, had a couple of tattoos of her own. The one on her shoulder read Clairebear, and had remained intact despite the accident. A more recent one, a rather strange symbol on her wrist that would be noted and photographed as part of her autopsy, had been partially peeled away and thus would cause much consternation for the detective who reexamined her case much later after speaking, or at least trying to speak, to what remained of the man who'd raped her sister.

Max made it to the top edge of the slope just as the slow-moving station wagon he'd passed near the prison pulled to a stop on the shoulder, its wide-eyed driver attempting to both shield the eyes of his elderly wife and call 9-1-1, all while pulling to a stop within feet of the bloody mess once known to police and others as Big Max Cody.

He could feel himself passing out, but Max really needed to see her. He lifted his chin and felt something in his neck give way, but managed to balance his head in that position just long enough to see her one last time.

Once again, Max just couldn't let it go.

They each had only one good eye, but they locked immediately in a fun house mirror kind of way, reflecting horrors neither could have expected.

Both of them would have been shocked to know, but shouldn't have been, that the same image flashed through their fading synapses at that very moment, before they each welcomed the darkness fast descending upon their consciousness.

Claire. After all, it was she who had brought them together.

If she could have spoken, the only thing she would have wanted to tell Big Max was her name. Melissa Williamson. Sister of Claire Williamson.

*You can't have everything,* she thought as she faded. *This will have to do.*

Melissa died as she planned; comforted by the image of her sister and the knowledge that she'd done her best to both end her suffering and take Max with her.

As for Max, his nightmare was just beginning.

# 2 MONTHS AFTER TOWY WEBSITE LAUNCH

Eyewitness 10 News Transcript

**VIDEO TOP STORY**

SHOOTOUT IN BROAD DAYLIGHT BETWEEN TOWY
"FARMERS" AND POLICE AT WILLOW CREEK MALL

**WELCOME**

Good evening, I'm Beth Montoya...
and I'm Mike Jennings...This is Eyewitness News.
Debra and John are off tonight...
-----------------------------------
**MALL SHOOTING**

BETH
Shots rang out near the southwest entrance of
Willow Creek Mall in downtown Greenville
today, sending dozens of office workers into a
panic during their lunch hour.
-----------------------------------
**WILLOW CREEK MALL**

BETH
Eyewitness news reporter Katy Nolan is live at
the scene with the latest. Katy?

KATY
Beth, no one was injured, but three suspects
were taken into custody after police received
a tip that the suspected operators of the
pirate website towy.la were in the area. What
happened next was shocking.

[VIDEO]

2259 They just started shooting. The cops
barely got out of their cars.

2267 I ran like hell, man. Them Towys are
(expletive deleted) crazy.

3531 It was chaos for a couple minutes, then
the shooters just stopped. One of them waved a
white rag and then it was over. Like it was
planned.

[LIVE]

KATY
The three shooters, whose names have not been
released, are apparently self-identified
"farmers", thusly named because they believe
they are cultivating and cleansing the lands
of evil, those who plan to follow the advice
posted on the Towy web site by killing someone
else, usually those judged to have escaped
punishment for serious crimes, before killing
themselves. Towy is an acronym, meaning "take
one with you." I spoke with Detective Thane
Parks earlier, who heads the local task force
in conjunction with the FBI.

[VIDEO]

KATY
Detective, who were the shooters and why did
they open fire?

PARKS
They're fans of the website that's been
  causing all this trouble. I don't know why

they did what they did, but it was pretty
stupid.

KATY
Have they been ID'd?

PARKS
No.

KATY
Is there any reason to believe the attack was
planned or coordinated with the founders of
the website?

PARKS
We don't know.

KATY
The ACLU says the founders of the site aren't
actually breaking any laws.

PARKS
No comment.

KATY
What can you comment on?

PARKS
If the founders are out there watching this,
I'll make a personal guarantee: Our system of
justice is going to work for you just like
it's worked for so many others. You know what
I mean. And if anyone has any information on
these kids, call the Greenville Police
Department and ask for Detective Parks.

KATY

Do you know they're kids, Detective? Do you
have names?

PARKS
What? No. Figure of speech.

KATY
Thank you, Detective.

PARKS
Yeah, right.

[LIVE]

KATY
No one knows yet who created the website that
has wrought so much havoc, but the FBI now
considers Greenville to be ground zero in the
hunt for the Towy founders. Katy Nolan,
Eyewitness News.

# Chapter Two

A couple years before Melissa Williamson met her end in a roadside ditch about twenty minutes west of Fairview, or eleven minutes if you're traveling over a hundred miles an hour, Charlie Sanderson, the person who unwittingly gave her the idea to kill Big Max, noticed his mother had started to hit the old Xanax even harder than before her breakdown.

It wasn't even a serious breakdown, more like a series of bad days really, but that didn't stop Charlie's stepdad from insisting that she up her intake so that, in his words, "we can have a little peace around here," which Charlie suspected was really just a way to both better control his mother and excuse his own indiscretions. The "we" was only his mom's husband, who himself was exceptionally tense. There was not a drug yet developed that could cure that particular family of what ailed them.

In Charlie's mind, the three of them would never be a family, anyway.

There had been other drugs before, all of them legal, which Charlie remembered even if his mother did not, and they had all been prescribed at the behest of Brad Connor, a man Charlie steadfastly refused to call Dad or Father or anything remotely warm and familial.

For all Charlie cared, Brad could fucking die.

Charlie's real father had been a mid-level accountant, a somewhat boring but hard-working man who always had a smile on his face no matter what was happening around him. Charlie's mom used to marvel at her husband as he handed over the last of their grocery money to the cashier at the local Safeway near the end of the month, cheerfully emptying his wallet a full week before payday.

They were never poor, exactly, just lower middle class, but there were many times his father had to pay the electric bill or other necessities with a credit card because his meager salary had not lasted a full month, usually because of an unexpected expense.

And it seemed there were always unexpected expenses.

Inevitably, the debt piled up, which became a source of tension between him and his wife that had not existed before. But that smile of his could usually melt her heart, and she was never able to stay mad at him for very long, regardless of their financial difficulties.

The Sanderson family always made do, and their little home never wanted for love and laughter. Neither Jim nor Anne ever let the sun go down on an argument, as Charlie's father explained to his son, and Charlie was determined to follow the same practice when he grew up and got married.

*If* he got married.

Charlie was a nerd and a loner, the former being something easily overcome in the days of such rapid technological advancements, even to be desired, but the latter was more problematic.

"One of these days you'll invent some code or website or something and make yourself a billion dollars," his mother would say, "but right now I want you to go out and make some friends not on the computer."

That was something Charlie had always found hard to do.

He was an only child, not by choice, but because of complications his mother suffered during his birth. He knew his mother wanted more children more than anything, not because she ever told him so, but because of the look in her eyes whenever she spoke with the parents of broods larger than her own. When Charlie had questioned her about it once, she looked really angry and then really sad, and gathered him in her arms and held him and cried for an hour. It was clear she didn't want him to feel guilty, which was indeed what Charlie felt, and no words ever passed between them on the subject again.

Because they struggled financially but were in a very good school district, Charlie had the distinction of feeling like the pauper at the wedding, never quite measuring up in terms of clothes or possessions, and as such was always slightly embarrassed about his status and appearance growing up.

In the first grade, one kid who rode the bus after school told a few of the others that Charlie had a hole in the back of his pants, with "his butt hanging out," and Charlie rode all the way to the last stop, way past his house, so that when he got off there would be fewer children to check his backside.

He never rode the bus again, unbeknownst to his parents, and walked to school every day thereafter, no matter the weather. It wasn't far, but he was often late, and at that age, the reputation for being difficult or different travels among the teachers almost as fast as the students. He began to see the teachers shake their heads sadly as he passed, like that beggar at the feast, which only intensified his alienation.

His grades were all A's, however, so the problems in school, at least elementary school, were mostly from the student body.

Charlie lived in his mind during those years, which was a very interesting place to be. He occasionally played with the kids in his neighborhood, who were always somehow more genial away from their peers at school, but he could also lie in the grass of his backyard for hours, staring at the clouds and having imaginary conversations with all kinds of wonderful playmates.

Once he spent an entire week in the summer of his tenth year talking to the son of Kurt Vonnegut about their fathers and writing and girls, about which Charlie had recently become obsessed, like most boys his age. He never bothered to find out whether the famous author actually had a son, but that didn't matter in the slightest within the realm of his imagination.

The following year, when his father died, everything changed.

Charlie was the one who found him, blue in the face one Saturday morning as his mother cooked breakfast for the three of them. His dad had been working lots of overtime, trying to get a little money saved, and normally would have been up and around, working on special projects as he did most Saturdays, but that day was different.

That Saturday, Charlie was going to try out for little league, something that both his parents saw as a good sign in terms of his socialization. Later that afternoon his father was going to the practice field for support, but he'd slept in, the first Saturday in weeks he'd done so, and Anne didn't want to disturb his rest.

They had argued the night before, about money of course, and she was feeling badly about it. She had suggested for the first time that he consider borrowing from a wealthy relative, an uncle they rarely saw, and the conversation had not gone well. She immediately regretted the idea, but something in his indignant reaction made backing down less enticing than moving forward, and so they fell into the trap of wounded pride and artifice, talking past each other until their voices could be heard all over the house and probably next door.

His mother slept in the living room that night, tossing and turning in the easy chair facing the television, finally falling asleep to a horrible infomercial about blankets with sleeves.

Charlie, who had listened to their argument from his room, crept into the bedroom where his father was sleeping and gently woke him up just after midnight.

"What is it, son?" he asked, instantly focused and awake.

"Nothing, Dad."

Charlie stood there, not knowing what to say or do.

"Talk to me, son."

After a long moment, Charlie was finally able to form his words.

"I know you don't want to call Uncle Teddy," he said, "but we could probably use the help."

It was such a simple thing to say, heartfelt and apologetic in tone, and Charlie could tell it made his father both immensely proud and terribly ashamed. He immediately regretted his words, but Jim Sanderson scooped his son up in his arms and hugged him tightly, something both of them had not actually done in quite a while, having recently graduated to handshakes and backslaps except for special occasions. It was a father-son cycle that only fathers and sons understand, one that ebbs and flows throughout life on a tide of masculinity, and one that neither of them would experience again after this night.

When he released his son, there were tears in Jim's eyes, something Charlie had never before witnessed, not even when his grandfather died, and at first he was even more scared and unsure than before.

But his father smiled that Jim Sanderson smile that so melted the heart of his wife and amused the grocery store checkers, and Charlie smiled back, and that was that. It was a moment they shared and seemed to understand without any more discussion, and Charlie went back to his room.

He went to sleep that night as happy as he had ever been, but he would end up haunted by those last words to his father for the rest of his life.

Charlie woke up early the next morning. He could see kitty-corner across the hall into his parents' bedroom. His dad had rolled out of bed again, and was fast asleep on the floor. Jim had gained a little weight during the last year, and usually snored like a truck driver, but that fact didn't register with Charlie at all, and he went back to sleep for another twenty minutes.

When he woke up, it was to the smell of bacon in the kitchen, and he padded out of his room and into the hall, where he could see his father was still sleeping in the same position as before.

Something didn't seem quite right, so Charlie went to where his father lay and touched his shoulder.

"Daddy, time to get up."

There was no response. His father was lying on his side, facing away from Charlie, so Charlie reached again for his father's shoulder and this time he shook him. Jim Sanderson rolled over, and his face was very dark.

The curtains were drawn, so Charlie flipped the light switch and turned back to his father. His skin looked blue, with lips an even darker, almost purple tint.

Still, Charlie was not fully aware of what had happened. It did not register to this highly intelligent boy of eleven that something momentous had occurred, something that would deeply affect him and alter the course of his life. All he knew was that, in his words to his mother, "Daddy won't wake up."

His mother was sitting in the chair she had slept in, reading the morning newspaper. When she looked into the eyes of her son, that was when Charlie knew his father was dead. He could tell by her eyes.

His mother jumped up and went to the back of the house, followed by her only child, and the two of them shared a moment no mother and son, or anyone, should ever have to share.

They looked down at the corpse of their husband and father.

"Call 9-1-1," she said, and sank to her knees, trying some crazy television version of CPR, to no avail. She was not crying, just working feverishly. Anne Sanderson was not generally one for histrionics. She was a doer, someone who saw a task to be performed and did what had to be done.

It was the words of her son from the hall that finally caused her to break down.

"My daddy's dead," Charlie said into the phone, as positive of that fact as he'd ever been of anything.

Anne burst into tears and ran to the phone.

"Please send an ambulance!" she yelled, and gave them the information they needed. As frantic as she sounded, she knew, as did her son, that there was no more need for CPR.

She left the line open and made the attempt as instructed, however, more out of duty than hope, until finally she told Charlie to hang up and help her move his father.

"What?"

"Help me move him," she said, and Charlie didn't question her again. The two of them each took an arm, and dragged his body out of the bedroom, down a short expanse of hall, through the kitchen, where the smell of bacon still filled the air, and into the living room, finally laying him beside the chair in which Anne had slept the previous night.

It was not a long distance, probably less than thirty feet, but it seemed to take forever, and several times Charlie had to stop, each time carefully putting one hand beneath his father's head so that it wouldn't bump against the floor. Then the two of them would straighten up, breathing hard, never looking directly at each other or the deceased, and somehow sensed when it was time to continue.

Charlie never asked his mother why she insisted the body be moved before the paramedics arrived; his thoughts were more on blaming himself for going back to sleep after first seeing his father on the floor.

The funeral was much as those things go, a blur of emotion and tears and relatives with food and awkward neighbors. There was a freshly stained wooden box sent from Jim's work containing a special bible, with a small insurance policy that enabled Anne to buy Charlie a computer, which changed the trajectory of his life, and the lives of a great many people afterwards, though not in the way that Charlie, or anyone, could have possibly imagined.

Charlie grew his hair long and became a handsome young man, a real head-turner, but he never quite escaped that inner lonely child, and thus lost himself in an online world, much as other kids do but not at all for the same reasons.

He and his mother became even closer after that, and were almost like best friends, at least until she met Brad, which was when everything really started to fall apart.

Brad owned what Charlie assumed was a shady insurance business, and he was slick and handsome and rich, everything his father was not, and it broke Charlie's heart when his mother took him aside and told him that they were to be married. Somehow that moment would be just as clear in his memory as the moment he saw the look in his mother's eyes the morning his daddy wouldn't wake up, and that only made him hate his stepfather more.

It was almost as if his mother had given up, held out as long as she could until her son could fend for himself, and at last decided, at seventeen, that Charlie would be okay if she took a husband.

It was not long after the wedding, that, still filled with fresh hatred and resentment he could never share, Charlie found a forum to vent his feelings.

The person he found to listen, or read what he had to say, was someone else who needed a virtual shoulder, a girl whose real name Charlie never knew until much later, who went by the screen name of `clairebear`.

# Chapter Three

No one would have ever guessed by looking at him that the little old man with the shy smile who spoke in the soft, cultured tones of a world traveler had once ordered the deaths of several dozen illiterate villagers deep in the jungles of Peru on little more than a whim, and worse. Nor would they have imagined that same man, at his advanced age, could have helped spark a global epidemic of bizarre homicides the likes of which the world had never seen.

Rodney Oscar Thomas, Mister Tee to those on staff at the Williamsburg Country Club with a sense of humor, which seemed to be restricted to those whose wages were earned hourly, was a genial old fellow who inspired no more fear in those he met than your average newborn kitten.

He was odd but amusing; seemingly harmless. But when his sordid past came to light in the months to come, his true nature would shock the world.

He was Chilean by birth, but adopted into a Peruvian family at the age of three after his father killed his mother in a fit of rage subsequent to his discovery of her in bed with his neighbor and his neighbor's wife and his neighbor's wife's sister. It was never known why the cuckold left the other members of the orgiastic enterprise alone, but the murderer was gone before his wife was cold and later presumed dead himself. The mountains into which he fled in the middle of winter were particularly inhospitable to those in such a rush to explore them that they would leave behind their coat.

TOWY Zero, as he would come to be called in the media some eighty years after his birth, was handed over to wealthy relatives of the man who'd last enjoyed the fruits of his poor mother and given the name Rodrigo Umberto Espinosa, as well as an upbringing as fine as could be hoped for in that part of the world in the years after the Great Depression and before World War II.

Chile was particularly hard hit economically, and little Rodrigo's new family was soon split up, with the boy sent to Lima, Peru to live with an uncle from his adopted family whose position in the military meant discipline and a better life than his adoptive parents could have ever hoped to provide in the port city of Arica.

He was later enrolled in military school and soon impressed both his uncle and instructors with his intelligence, fine marksmanship, and exceptional leadership abilities.

In his spare time the boy read and studied and mostly kept to himself, except for excursions into the Andean hills to capture and torture to death small animals, eventually working his way up to a nameless younger child he'd managed to lure away from one of the poor neighborhoods near downtown.

Rodrigo also was quite skilled at keeping secrets.

It was years later, as a Lieutenant General battling the terrorist group Shining Path under the direction of President Fujimori, that all of little Rodrigo's skills finally came together. He was now known as a particularly ruthless purveyor of punishment upon those who ran afoul of his superiors, and seemed to almost enjoy the suffering of his enemies, whether actual or imagined.

The rise of Shining Path in the 80's and Fujimori's death squads in the early 90's was just an example, as Rodrigo saw it, of being in the right place at the right time.

It was not long after Rodrigo led a small, secretive offshoot of Grupo Colina into the mountains in search of two suspected terrorists who were never found, slaughtering villagers on the way, that two truck bombs went off on Tarata Street in Lima, an upscale district of the city.

As a result, El Culo de Arica, as he was now informally known to both the men under his command and the terrorists he was assigned to kill, was unleashed with a vengeance.

He liked his nickname better in English, which he spoke fluently and with almost no accent. The Asshole of Arica just had that alliterative flair, and some even thought he had come up with it himself since, given his background, he would have been the only person to know the city of his birth, but what no one ever questioned was its legitimacy.

Rodrigo had indeed grown up to be an asshole. What he had still managed to hide from the world was the fact that he was also a sociopath.

Until La Cantuta Massacre. Less than seventy-two hours after the bombings, Rodrigo and his men burst into a dormitory at the Enrique Guzmán y Valle National Education University, also known as La Cantuta, and kidnapped nine students and a teacher.

None of the abductees were ever heard from again.

Even his men were shocked at what they were ordered to do, but to the Asshole of Arica, information and interrogation seemed beside the point. Of course everyone knew the students had to die, but the manner of their demise was so terrifically gruesome that two of his men actually refused to continue and were immediately shot in the head by the Asshole himself, who then ordered the others to continue the grisly torture for his own amusement.

They did as they were told.

In the years after the prosecutions and the amnesty and then the repeal of the amnesty, two more of the soldiers involved "committed suicide" and the others somehow never told anyone how, after his men had interrogated and tortured the students, the Asshole of Arica had methodically sliced open one of them as he writhed in pain and fed the innards to his friend, suffocating him in the process, just as he'd done to the animals in the forest as a boy.

Even the president of Peru eventually went to jail as a result of the massacre, but few of the men there ever spoke of what they'd seen to anyone, being either too frightened or too certain they would not be believed, or both.

Rodrigo himself managed to publicly feign outrage at the massacre, even appearing to be on the side of justice, which led to death threats and his forced emigration, something he'd hoped for all along.

He was able to leave the country just before the release of damning documents released by a group of anonymous military officers, changing his name and appearance and, for all intents and purposes, ceasing to exist in terms of his adopted country's war on terrorism.

That was something even the men who witnessed his atrocities could not have possibly imagined, but as is sometimes the case with such things, the powers that be had bigger fish to fry.

Rodrigo Umberto Espinosa had become a ghost.

He traveled through life from Chile to Peru to Argentina to America, occasionally indulging in his dark pastime, but he was always very clever and very careful and was never really bothered or even paid much mind by others, despite the monster that he was. So when he found himself a member of the Williamsburg Country Club, where all anyone ever saw was a sweet old man who smiled and tipped well and swam early each morning, mostly before any other club members had arrived, it was simply the expected penultimate chapter of the darkly charmed life to which he had grown accustomed.

What he did not know, nor could have even imagined, was that there was one other person who would soon know his secret, and that person would rouse his inner monster once more.

***

To say Jesus Two Bears was a young man of mixed descent was like saying El Culo de Arica was an old man with a secret. Both were grand and sweeping understatements truly appreciated only by their subjects.

JT, as he preferred to be called, was born to a Lakota Sioux father and a Yaqui-Mexican mother in the back of a Volkswagen camper parked in a lot which served both the Catholic church to the north and a dive bar to the east, just off Road No. 1 in the tiny town of Pantisuth, MI.

A clinic and nurse practitioner's office on the other side of the store and church, respectively, were both locked up and dark for reasons never quite understood beyond the fact that it was the night *before* Christmas Eve, which wasn't a holiday even to the local Catholics.

JT's father always told his son that he was named after his grandfather who had been involved in the incident at Wounded

Knee and gone stark raving mad, but his mother told a completely different story.

"I was hurtin' pretty bad, but your pops was so damn drunk I did'n trust him to drive around and find a hospital. He was nervous, y'see, cause you was our first. So's I kept makin' him go check that clinic to see if anyone come 'round, but in between was that booze bar, and you know your daddy."

At that point in the story JT would always laugh, more out of respect than anything else. He'd probably heard the story a hundred different times. His mother always enjoyed talking about his father after he passed, said it made her feel close to him, and whenever he had the chance to make his mother happy, JT took it.

"So's I was screamin' bloody murder, jus' cussin' him a blue streak, and he'd leave me alone and go check the clinic. But we both knew what your father was doin'."

"I knew, mama?" he'd ask, as he always did.

"Oh, you knew, son," she'd cackle, reflexively rubbing her belly. "Trus' me, you knew."

What it boiled down to was the last time he came back to the camper, his father's face was as white as the snow on the ground outside, and he began frantically searching for the keys so he could drive away.

"What'choo doin' you dumb sonuvabitch?" his wife screamed.

"They's after me!" he shouted back. "Couple of big 'uns!"

"What the fuck you talkin' about you crazy bastard?"

JT's mother swore like a sailor even then, a habit that never diminished with age.

"Bears!" his father screamed. "Jesus!"

The entire camper went quiet then, as if the air had suddenly been sucked out of it like a punctured balloon. JT's father was nearly weeping, trying to find his keys, and his mother, who was very close to giving birth, was suddenly unsure if what her husband said was complete bullshit from the bottle, or actually true. It was a fairly remote area and bears were certainly not outside the realm of possibility.

"Then there's this scratchin' at the door," she whispered, like an old fabler across a campfire.

At this point in the story, JT's eyes usually grew wide, not out of artifice, but because he would by then be genuinely entranced by the story. His mother should have been an actress.

"Your father turns to me, his face like death itself, and then...wham! The door flies open!"

JT always jumped when she whammed him. Even though he knew it was coming, he couldn't help but flinch.

"And sonuvabitch if it wasn't a bear!" she laughed. "Only it was really just a doctor from the clinic all dressed up in his big winter coat an' hat."

They always laughed together at that point, a little sadly, as the end of the story was close and always a little melancholy.

"You came out so nice and easy your father hadn't even sobered up when they put you in his arms. He named you Two Bears 'cause of those two big 'uns he thought he saw, not your grandfather. And not only was there not two bears, there wasn't even two doctors. Your pops was just so damn drunk he was seein' double."

JT and his mother would laugh again, this time a little less enthusiastically, and then his mother would end the story.

"He kept askin' an' askin' where the other doctor was so he could thank him, too, so the one what found us finally borrowed a pair of glasses from the nurse and pretended to be the other bear."

His father died in their home on the Pine Ridge Rez at the southern edge of the South Dakota Badlands, not far from Wounded Knee, where he swore to his dying breath that JT's grandfather had taken a stand against evil in the world.

"I 'spect the same from you, son."

Those were the last words JT ever heard his father say. He was thirteen years-old.

JT's mother lived all the way until his sixteenth birthday, at which time he could finally take to the road and see what the world had to offer him, but it was, in the end, his grandfather who finally caught up to him to make sure he'd take the stand against evil his own father had always implored.

JT bummed around the country for over a year before ending up in a sweat lodge with two wealthy Anglos who liked the nice, polite kid with the great story about his name, and who just happened to be members of a country club that was looking to hire a new pool attendant.

"Good benefits," the man told JT, "medical and dental."

The former turned out to be both useless and of utmost importance at the same time, because JT was carrying a disease that was the real cause of his grandfather's death, Wounded Knee or no. A disease that his father carried but never developed, and which normally killed its host less than two years after symptoms developed, which included terrible insomnia, hallucinations, and dementia.

It explained a lot about the family stories of his grandfather, actually.

While there was no cure for fatal familial insomnia, having health insurance for the first time in his life at least enabled JT to discover what his future held, which ended up giving him a chance to take that stand against evil, just like his daddy wanted.

Every morning, rain or shine, he opened up the pool room at the Williamsburg Country Club, and every morning he looked into the face of evil, also known as Mister Tee to all with a sense of humor, which, fortunately, or perhaps unfortunately, Jesus Two Bears had inherited from his mother to go along with the gene that would take his life, which he got from his father and his father before him.

For a long while JT was as ignorant of Mister Tee's history as Charlie Sanderson was of Melissa and her sister and Big Max, but it would not be long before the lives of them all would be forever entwined, and their secrets revealed to all.

In spite of what the world would later discover they all had in common, it would be JT who would come to be known as the Pioneer. The very first TOWY.

Though he would never know that, if he had, JT would have also known that his father, and his grandfather before him, would have been proud he had taken his stand.

# 1 YEAR, 9 MONTHS AFTER TOWY WEBSITE

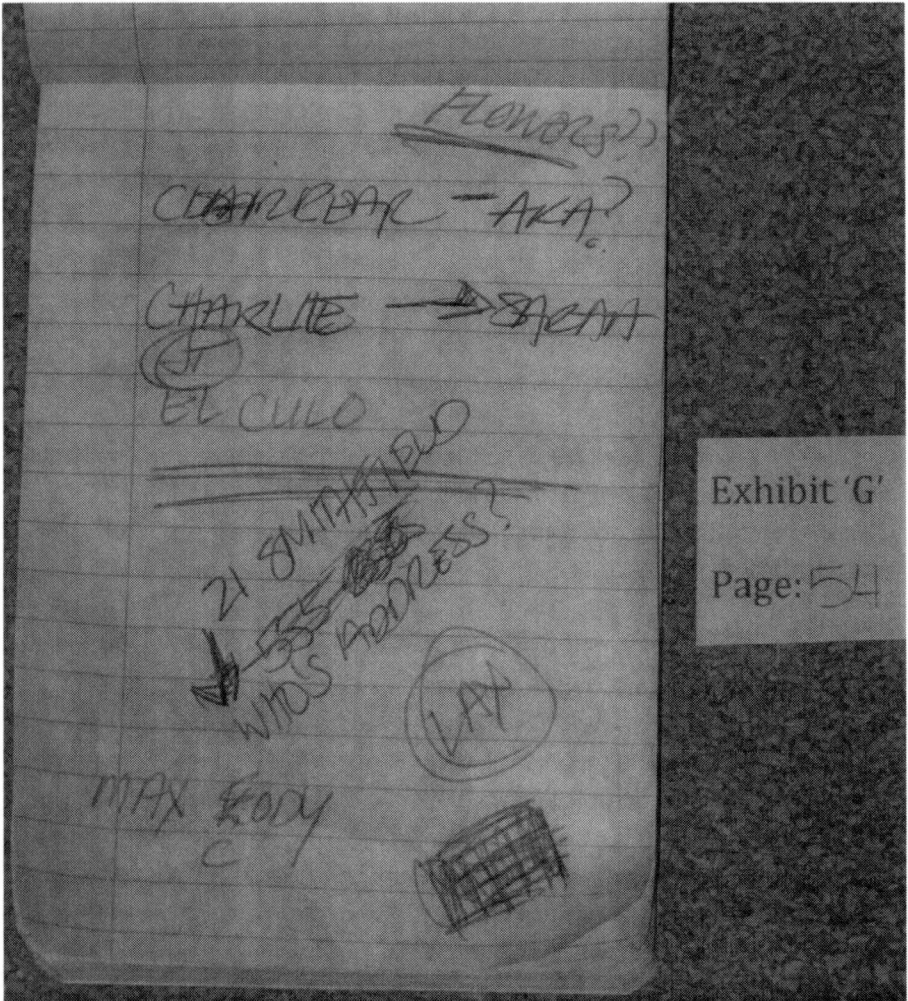

**Grand Jury Exhibit 'G'**
**Officer Anita Hellstrom's Notebook From Vehicle Console**

# **Chapter Four**

It was getting harder and harder for Sarah's mother to keep her daughter out of jail.

Sarah herself wasn't particularly concerned. She had always been very good at figuring people out, especially when it came to the line between sympathy and exasperation and exactly how far she could use the former to delay or completely forestall the latter.

But even Sarah understood a lot of that changed when she turned eighteen.

Men were easiest, of course. Ironically, the older they were, the better. A lot of the grandpas were just that, grandfatherly, although she suspected, and she would have been right, that the perv never dies within the loins of man. She was pretty sure more than a few of those geezers went home to pop a pill and give it to grandma hard and heavy while imagining her face in their lap, an image that never failed to both fascinate and repulse her.

It always made her think of her cherry-popper, a British exchange student almost five years her senior who'd taken one look at the fifteen year-old state senator's daughter and pronounced her "flat out bangin'" and then proceeded to do just that as often as he could sneak past the dogs at her parents' estate.

She'd quickly grown tired of his inane blather, which seemed to revolve almost exclusively around her "tight box and rock n roll tits", another of his rude expressions whose charm eluded her.

Sarah found men tiresome after that, and in spite of her somewhat slutty reputation at school, due mainly to a small, jealous clique of equally wealthy but much less intelligent fashionistas, she would not do the deed for several more years.

Which didn't mean her charms went to waste.

The younger cops were next behind the grandpas, still easy because they were usually arrogant enough that they thought they could actually get her. But like the envious heathers from the private academy her father insisted she attend, their IQs were usually in the range of room temperature.

If you lived in the Yukon.

Worst of all, naturally, were the ladies. No amount of guile ever seemed enough to completely erase her long, chestnut hair and perfect teeth, along with an athletic figure most of them would have given their career for. Indeed, had they looked like Sarah, they would have never gone into law enforcement at all. A thought that crossed more than one mind as reports were being written in vain before the inevitable call from the senator's chief of staff reminding them there was even more to resent the little bitch for.

Had just one of them actually taken an interest in what Sarah had to say, they would have discovered a preternaturally mature young woman who was, to put it simply, too smart for her own good.

She'd been obsessed with suicide ever since she was a child, after finding old albums filled with newspaper clippings, letters, and other evidence that some serious mental illness flowed through the females on her mother's side of the family.

Her great-great grandmother Alice lost her husband not to the Great War, but to the influenza pandemic that swept through the ranks of the newly mobilized as they geared up for the battlefields of Europe. He died on Armistice Day as the rest of the country celebrated, breathing his last to a first year medical student in a tent city near Boston Harbor, still waiting to ship out.

Alice checked into the honeymoon suite of the Waldorf Astoria in New York City on Christmas Eve, threw wide the casement windows and lay down on the bed to await her wintry dissolution, which came mercifully quickly. Her infant child was found under a coat in the closet by a chambermaid several hours after her mother's body had been removed, the baby girl still sleeping and warm as toast.

That baby grew up to birth sixteen children, seven of whom were killed in a fire their mother was suspected of setting; nothing was ever proved, and she lived to the ripe old age of ninety-seven, as dotty as a shithouse rat to the end.

Sarah's grandmother was also long-lived, and the only one of the ancients Sarah met personally. She was also the sanest, and Sarah loved her dearly. As a child she spent several summers at the old woman's house, which smelled of oatmeal cookies and baby oil, and Granny Slaton would regale her with stories of her days with Sarah's grandfather after World War II.

Sarah loved the old woman so much that she became terrified her grandmother would die right under her nose, and so used to sneak into her bedroom after she'd gone to sleep and listen in the doorway until she made sure the old woman was still breathing. Sometimes she'd wait for hours until she was absolutely certain, and then trudge back to bed as the sun rose.

She didn't find out until much later that Granny Slaton almost never slept through the night, and had very likely been wide-awake as her granddaughter worried over her.

Perhaps the old woman wasn't as sane as all that.

By the time Granny Slaton actually got a good night's sleep, she never woke up, and while Sarah could never be sure if she had actually been standing in her grandmother's doorway just watching the woman at the moment of her death, she certainly blamed herself as if she had.

It was the summer of her sixth year, the summer all her nightmares and obsessions were born. The summer of ideas, ideas that would eventually impact the world.

After that first sexual relationship, Sarah forgot all about boys and focused on computer science, then coding, and then hacking, which is why her father was constantly risking his career to try and keep his daughter out of jail. She started small, poking around into various state agencies' email systems to see what people were saying about her father (he was almost universally liked and respected) and finally branching out into the lives and bank accounts of her neighbors.

She stole passport numbers and sold them to Ukrainians, dabbled in hardware virtualization, and even traveled to Europe for the weekend at the age of sixteen for a Black Hat security conference on the county dime, not that the county knew about it. Most of the time she left no traces of her work, but it was always with the neighbors that she got sloppy.

Even so, none of this really engaged her; Sarah had developed the attention span of a five year-old with ADHD.

Speaking of which, she also sold Oxycontin prescriptions for a while.

Not all of her pastimes were illegal. She took to trolling the Internet to embarrass guys who preyed on vulnerable women, allowing them to do most of the work as she watched with bemusement.

Sarah idolized her father, who was incredibly busy except for when she was in trouble, and she resented her mother those crazy and often suicidal ancestors who she couldn't seem to rid from her mind. She knew she was troubled and didn't care; she knew her crimes were cries for attention, but it didn't matter.

She would usually cooperate up to a certain point when caught, just to get a feel for police procedure in case she decided to continue her malfeasance into her adult years, but she always held back just enough to provide both herself and any others she'd managed to drag into her crimes a certain level of plausible deniability that even the cops had to respect.

And of course, when she crossed into exasperation territory, she could always bat her eyes and wiggle her ass.

Except with the women.

"Sugar, don't pull that crap with me."

Margaret Swanson, the assistant chief of police since old man Perry retired and everyone got promoted up, sat across her desk from the snotty Crane bitch and smiled. She knew the little cunt hated to be called Sugar or Sweetie or Honey or Baby or anything that smelled chauvinistic or condescending in any way.

*No, being condescending is your job, isn't it Sweetie?*

"Mister Deauville is going to press charges this time," she added smugly.

Sarah shrugged. Large Marge wasn't worth wasting her breath on and was almost as irritating as those stupid guys that tried to pick her up online. *Yeah, like I'm really going to fly out and*

*meet some unemployed mechanic with BO and grease under his*
*fingernails or some hipster doofus writing his thesis on the*
*Exigency of Celebrity Gossip in a Post-Recessionary Economy.*

"And your daddy won't be able to give me any headaches, neither."

Sarah's eyes flashed in anger for the first time. Too bad her father would have never actually harassed anyone just for doing their job; he was so much better than that.

That was half the problem, really. Sarah could never measure up, not in her own mind.

But most cops would have known better than to even mention such a possibility.

Especially since her father died only a few short months prior, as Sarah sat in the exact same seat.

***

It had been a very long legislative session, and a very late night at the state capital building on the night the senator died. He staggered back to his office with nary an aide in sight, as he'd been working his staff incredibly hard for weeks, and as the light at the end of the tunnel was now in view, he figured he could coast the rest of the way under his own steam, for a change.

That had always been his least favorite part of the job; depending on staff who basically gave up their lives in the service of his career. Oh sure, they loved their jobs and many had gone on to careers in politics themselves, but he could see the toll it took on their families even if they couldn't, which was ironic given the fact that he'd only recently begun to notice the toll it was taking on his own family.

It had been so easy in the beginning, to make excuses and soldier on "for the people", but he'd been kidding himself. It was a selfish game the way he'd played it, and he'd finally decided to do something about it.

The senator was going to retire.

He hadn't told a soul, especially since there had been so much talk about running for governor in two years. If he'd breathed a word to anyone, all hell would have broken loose in the party, and his final, meager achievements before the recess would have been scuttled for those legislators whose ambitions were still corruptible. He wasn't even sure his family would want him to quit, and they were the ones who suffered the most from his work, if living in luxury could be described in any known universe as remotely resembling suffering.

Except for Sarah. Sarah would understand. Oh, he could imagine her tough exterior hanging together for a while as she assessed his seriousness, but once she understood exactly what was going to happen, she'd crumble. The hard façade she had built around herself over the years would melt away and reveal his little girl once more. At least, that was his hope.

She was actually the catalyst of his change of heart, something he was sure she'd find supremely hilarious when he told her.

*High-larious, Dad,* she'd say in that sarcastic tone she seemed to reserve for all things related to her father. If they spoke at all, that is. It seemed like the only time they communicated the last couple of years was at some local constabulary, as he was bailing or talking or threatening or cajoling or promising her way out of one bit of trouble or another. He didn't know where she got all of that anger, but he wasn't so blind as to think himself innocent or unaware that his child was spiraling out of control.

Still, it was easy to solve the immediate crisis and then move on, basking in the relative quiet between storms and losing himself in his work. It was simply *the way things were,* and it was an awfully hard path to turn back.

Until one of his colleagues had come home to find his son hanging from a hook in the back of his wife's closet, inches above her thousand dollar Manolo Blahnik pumps.

It was the shoes that got him. He wasn't even sure how he'd heard that detail; it certainly wasn't his colleague. Probably a staffer's gossip had crossed some invisible line between poor taste and downright venom, but it didn't matter. He couldn't get that image out of his head. The juxtaposition was perfectly horrendous.

Perfectly apt. Perfect.

On the night he died, the senator was looking forward to catching some shut-eye on the overstuffed couch in his outer office before the final vote in the morning, after which he was going to begin some important legislating back home. Putting his family back together.

Sarah had been a real handful lately, and in spite of her weekly tantrum about him not paying attention to her, or because of it, really, he couldn't wait to give lie to that particular complaint as his first order of business.

It was this excitement that probably killed him, as he was actually awake when the text came in. His aide had shut down the phones and the senator was so tired that he probably wouldn't have heard his cell if he'd made it into REM sleep, but he was going over the conversation with Sarah in his mind when the familiar text tone interrupted his reverie.

He looked at his phone.

**`assholes giving me shit again`**

He had to laugh at those words next to the picture of his little girl. Sarah's avatar was from when she was four years old. Such a beautiful child. Such a potty mouth.

He looked at the time. He could make it upstate in a couple of hours, do whatever needed to be done, and then just hop a morning puddle jumper in for the early session. Sarah would be completely shocked he didn't let her stew until tomorrow evening, given the calendar. Maybe she'd even take the flight back with him. It would be nice to show her around one last time and then tell her his plans.

He texted her back.

**`on my way`**

He added 'I love you' in Morse code, spelling out the dots and dashes, something he hadn't done since she was a little girl. It had always been their little secret from her mother, a fun remnant from his Navy days. Even if she'd forgotten how to read it, she'd remember the meaning.

He grabbed his coat and was out the door, laughing at the look he imagined on her face if she'd managed to see the text before they took her phone away.

Sarah's mother was nowhere nearly as effective at damage control as her husband had always been, which was just another thing for which she could be blamed by Sarah. She wanted to blame his death on her, too, but even Sarah couldn't bring herself that low.

Her parents had been talking on the phone when her father had missed the curve and careened off the road just half an hour from the jail. As Senator Crane figured, the police had called his wife and she had decided to wait until morning to fill him in, and had thus been taken completely by surprise at his call. She hadn't even been aware that their call had been tragically cut off, but simply assumed they'd lost the signal and went back to sleep.

Given the circumstances, all charges were dropped, of course. Even in death, the senator had considerable pull with the local police.

No one ever knew, until much later, why the senator had decided to drive back in the middle of the night to do what he could have probably accomplished with a phone call, or certainly assigned to a local attorney.

Every night since, Sarah had imagined killing herself, but instead ended up only implementing new ways to cause herself problems, as if being in jeopardy might actually bring him back. But as he wasn't coming back anytime soon, the whole situation was basically an exercise in futility. The only reason she got in trouble in the first place was to spend time with him.

***

Marge immediately knew she'd fucked up, but there was nothing she could say or do to take it back. The bitch had her now. She sighed and started tearing up her report.

*Fuck me.*

They both knew that Marge's slip of the tongue was Sarah's get-out-of-jail-free card, and she would play it. Oh, how she'd play it.

Because Sarah was most definitely not her father's daughter. And that was the other half of the problem.

**AP**

**The Associated Press** ⊘
@AP

News, discussion and a behind-the-scenes look at the process from The Associated Press. Managed 24/7 by a team of editors based in NY: apne.ws/APStaff
Global · ap.org

| 62,905 | 7,003 | 2,484,646 |
|--------|-------|-----------|
| TWEETS | FOLLOWING | FOLLOWERS |

👤▾  ✈ Follow

**Tweets** All / No replies

AP **The Associated Press** @AP
TOWY "farmers" now estimated at over 2 million worldwide    34 min
apne.ws/19dilsme

📄 View summary          ← Reply  ⇄ Retweet  ★ Favorite  ••• More

# Chapter Five

"I can hack his email account if you want."

Charlie had, of course, already done so.

Anne just looked at her son. She was vaguely aware of how unhappy Charlie had been ever since she'd married Brad, but more and more she'd found ways to dull her own pain that had probably been blinding her to just how separate he'd become.

"I don't think that's a good idea, Charlie," she said carefully, not wanting to start an argument. They never argued when Jim was alive. They'd been a family then. What they were now was something else entirely.

"He's cheating on you, Mom," Charlie said. He knew this to be true from the emails of course, but couldn't say so. Subconsciously she knew he was right, but Anne had not yet been able to face the reality of her irreparably broken marriage.

She slapped him, causing his eyes to grow wide and his jaw to go slack. His mother had never once hit him in all his years. Charlie was almost happy about it; at least it showed signs of life, but the look of absolute devastation in his mother's eyes made it too hard to be happy about much of anything.

"I'm sorry," he whispered, almost like a prayer, but there was no taking back the words that had hurt her so. No act of contrition could ever undo what he'd done in a simple moment of frustration. The look in his mother's eyes was a look of utter worthlessness, and Charlie would have gladly given life and limb if he could reverse time and take it all back. What made it worse was that he knew his mother wanted the very same thing.

She lowered her head in her hands and began to cry.

Charlie tried everything, but she was inconsolable. His stepfather had made his mother feel increasingly bad about herself over the last couple of years, and try as he did to cheer her up, Charlie knew at some point there was a line that had been crossed, and even her only child could not bring her back. For the first time in his life he understood what a soul mate really was, because he knew that his father had been that for her. Losing her husband had taken something from deep inside that not even Charlie could ever replace.

She had her good days, of course, but for the most part the bad days began to overwhelm her. Where once he had been able to elicit a laugh with one of the jokes they'd shared from when he was a boy, it seemed like her smiles were mere ghostly representations of a time in their lives that would never return. His suggestion of what they both knew, that her marriage was a sham, seemed not to be something from which she would ever recover.

"Bessie's out of her tank, Mom!"

Anne looked up from her newspaper at her son. She'd read the same story several times now and couldn't seem to grasp what it meant. Charlie was smiling down at her hopefully, with that same expression that made her so sad every time she saw it cross his face. It was in his eyes, something no mother should ever have to see in her child.

It was pity.

She tried to focus on what he was saying, but suddenly she was taken back to that terrible Saturday years ago, looking up at her eleven year-old son.

*"Daddy won't wake up."*

*She was sitting in the chair she had slept in, reading the morning newspaper, and when she looked into the eyes of her son, that was when she knew that her husband was dead.*

*Anne jumped up and went to the back of the house, followed by her only child, and the two of them shared a moment no mother and son, or anyone, should ever have to share.*

*They looked down at the body of her husband and his father.*

"Mom, what are you doing?" Charlie screamed, and she was jolted from her memory.

Anne was standing in the middle of her bedroom, staring at the empty bed.

"What's happening?" She looked at Charlie, and there was only fear, because he knew that she had been, for a moment, completely lost inside her head, which they both knew was an increasingly dangerous place to be.

Charlie guided her back to the living room and didn't attempt to remind her of the joke they'd shared about Bessie, his tarantula that she had, against every ounce of better judgment, allowed him to get after the death of his father. She had worried that he'd developed a morbid fascination with death around that time, looking up terrible things on his new computer and behaving oddly. She considered taking him to a therapist, concerned that he might develop suicidal thoughts or urges, but he seemed to calm down a bit after he got the spider, as if his interests were a wide-cast net that he'd learned to focus more narrowly in order to catch whatever prey he'd been looking for.

Their Bessie joke had been the first bit of humor they'd shared after her husband died, the first time laughter had returned to their home, and Charlie's mother had loved the crazy spider for that.

He'd found Bessie on the Internet, and she'd let him buy the arachnid and a terrarium for his room. It was only a month after the death of his father, and though she hated the thing initially and would have preferred a dog or even a goldfish, she had always recognized the fact that her son was unique, and she indulged him. She had to admit it looked rather delicate and even beautiful at times, as long as it wasn't moving. She cringed to see those spindly legs in operation, but that was just the sort of thing that little boys think are cool, and Charlie spent hours and hours in his room, watching Bessie in fascination. The females supposedly lived much longer than the males, something she could never bear to tease him about, given the circumstances.

So it had been a shock when her son emerged from his room and told her that his spider had escaped its enclosure.

"What?" she very nearly screamed. "Oh my God!"

And then she saw him smile; an event that had been all too rare of late, and she knew that she'd been had.

Her jaw dropped and then she got the giggles, which turned into laughter, which morphed into something akin to real guffaws. For a while she could hardly breathe, and it was infectious. The two of them laughed until they cried. Charlie actually doubled over and collapsed into her lap like a child, and though he was much too big for it, she held him in her arms and rocked him like a baby until their laughter subsided.

It seemed like they'd reached a milestone in their life after Jim, the first time either one of them really felt safe since he'd passed. They felt *close*, an intimacy they'd not shared since Charlie was a baby, and the bond forged that day around the circumstance of a silly joke had lasted until the day she no longer responded in the usual way. The day she forgot herself and her son and everything they'd gone through together.

Charlie had never failed to get a smile out of his mother, or been facetiously directed to stay in his room until he ran across his creepy pet, until that day. The day he lost any hope of bringing her back to her old self.

And he desperately wanted to do just that. It had been his single-minded obsession for months.

For the first time, Charlie knew he would never be his father. His mother had chosen another man, his hated stepfather, and the full weight of that choice had never borne down on him until the moment that his mother didn't recognize his attempt to save her.

Charlie began to withdraw from the world, much as his mother had done, and though he knew where he was headed, he was unable to stop himself. Like a train that had jumped the tracks, there was only one place his journey was going to end.

It really was similar to what he'd read about people who'd been in car accidents, when time had slowed and the impact, while inevitable, was both minutely observable and inescapable. Charlie was trapped in that 'moment before,' the instant when you know something very bad is going to happen and all you can do is watch and wait.

It was while he was waiting that he met a girl named Sarah and introduced her to his other online friend, `clairebear`.

# 1 YEAR, 11 MONTHS AFTER TOWY WEBSITE

REUTERS News at 6:08 p.m. EDT

NEW YORK CITY (AP) – The United Nations formally announced the establishment of a special advisory commission to deal with the worldwide phenomenon known as the TOWY crisis, appointing former Surgeon General of the United States William Bradford Chase as its head. The Advisory Commission on TOWY Neutralization and Opposition Worldwide, or ACTNOW, will hold meetings beginning next week while the General Assembly is in session, with permanent commission members to be named in conjunction with recommendations from The Second and Third Committees. The TOWY crisis has now claimed almost thirteen thousand lives globally, including both perpetrators and random victims, but the exponential increase in deaths over the past three months and the recent incident during Congressional hearings has raised its profile among member nations, leading to the dissolution of the TOWY Ad Hoc Committee in favor of a semi-permanent commission. The practice, which originated in the United States, has now spread to almost every corner of the globe through social media in less than **two years**, and the suicide rates in some areas have more than doubled.

# **Chapter Six**

In the weeks after she'd slapped her son for the first time in
his life, Anne Sanderson seemed to fall into an even deeper
depression. She knew deep down that Charlie was probably right
about her husband; there had been far too many late nights at the
office and business trips that were extended over a weekend.

But she didn't want to know.

It was as if she was trapped in some horrible soap opera,
filled with the requisite extra-marital clichés and tropes and it had
all been scripted and timed down to the second and there would be
no deviations even if she found the strength to rouse herself from
her stupor, which she most certainly could not do.

It was painful for her and painful for her son, but all she
could do was watch and wait and hope for it all to end.

Charlie grew more morose by the day. He spent almost all of
his time ensconced in his room at the computer, and there was no
one to bring him out of his shell. At least, no one his mother knew
about.

\*\*\*

**r u fukn srs?**

Charlie blinked. He wasn't sure what to type in response to
this girl, as usual. She was like no one he'd ever met, well, "met" if
you counted Internet forums in general and sites for people
suffering from depression in particular. For all he knew she was
some fat, forty-seven year-old hermaphrodite from Cleveland
instead of a hot young computer hacker from the next state over.

For some reason, he chose to take her avatar at face value,
which was a thumbnail of a girl with long brown hair and dark,
intense eyes who seemed to be everywhere Charlie looked these

days, which was mostly in chat rooms filled with some of the saddest people he'd ever encountered.

He'd seen the same user name on three or four different sites over several months before he dared address her. Charlie was a lurker, mostly, fascinated by the exquisite suffering of anonymous strangers. Sometimes he googled their screen names and tried to figure out as much as he could about their lives if their stories interested him. So many people with tragedy and suffering in their lives, all looking for solace in the posts of electronic strangers.

Some said misery loves company and some said that people starving in North Korea didn't affect one's appetite whatsoever. Charlie wasn't sure, but there was something about the forums that kept him hanging on.

Something about *her*.

She was outrageous and outspoken and had been banned from two sites that he knew of because of her behavior. Nonetheless, she intrigued him. Even when she was rude and downright unkind, there was something about her insight that cut through the usual blather like a knife and got to the heart of the problem. A humanity that could not be denied.

Empathy, he thought, although from her bitterly caustic persona, he would never have accused her of such a thing. And he could tell, to her, it would be just that.

An accusation.

Once Charlie stayed up all night watching an amazing thread in which **unwanted_image** seemed to talk a desperate woman from the Midwest out of killing herself and her disabled child. Charlie didn't know whether others had attempted to call the authorities or contact the owners of the website, but for several hours it felt like just the three of them, the despondent woman, her unlikely savior, and himself, observing from the shadows. The moderators were all but useless; even those supposedly trained to deal with such people eventually hung back and allowed the anti-troll to work her magic.

Not long after that was when he first "spoke" to her, with an offhand and indirect comment on a subject long forgotten. She had responded immediately, not allowing him to remain on the periphery of the conversation, as was his practice.

**wtf d u kno abt it?** were her first words to him, a phrase they would eventually share as a kind of milestone in their friendship, much like the tarantula-on-the-loose joke Charlie and his mother had shared.

Even then, he never quite knew how to respond.

**r u fukn srs?**

His fingers hovered over the keyboard. He was always overly cautious with her, for some reason. Hell, he knew the reason. It was as obvious as the bristles on Bessie's back. Just another defense mechanism.

**u thr chikless?**

He didn't like it when she got too aggressive and now it was directed at him. She was like a powder keg, filled with a rage for which she never sought help from the others. Her participation appeared to be strictly one-sided, only as a commenter, never a confessor, although Charlie suspected the truth was that commentary was her therapy. He saw subtle hints the others in her threads seemed to miss beneath her rough, bombastic exterior. Clues that told him her problems might not be all that dissimilar to his own.

☺

That was unexpected. In all of his time observing her online, he had never seen her post such a symbol. She was definitely not an emoticon-type girl.

Charlie couldn't help himself.

He typed: **lol**

She responded quickly: **cheesdick**

**That's more like it.** he replied. Charlie, unlike most teenagers and possibly most human beings who texted, generally disliked abbreviations and shortcuts and the lack of grammar and capitalization so inherent in electronic communication, whether it was on his phone or in forums.

There was a long pause, too long for Sarah, and for a moment he thought he'd lost her. He'd spent months cultivating their relationship, such as it was, and he'd been waiting for this moment, and he'd blown it. At that instant he realized that he had actually thought of little else for a very long time.

**unwanted_image** had been his savior just as surely as that woman from Minnesota with the disabled kid, and he'd completely fucked it up.

"Shit."

He waited. Nothing.

He was about to slam his keyboard when she finally responded.

**call me**

"Whoa."

**What's your number?**

He almost added a snarky sobriquet at the end, but decided against it. If she was actually reaching out to him in the real world, maybe she needed a friend.

She did.

They spoke on the phone for hours that night. It was the first real conversation Charlie had had in weeks. Her story spilled out like a river, long dammed and ready to rock and roll. And it turned out that Charlie had been right.

Aside from their personalities and general areas of interest, they actually had quite a bit in common.

*** 

On the night his mother decided to kill herself, Charlie was two hundred miles away meeting Sarah face-to-face for the very first time. It never occurred to Anne that her son would realize immediately that she had picked that night on purpose because he was away; she was a little too far gone for that. Ironically, had she not been more doped up than usual on anti-depressants, she might have chosen another night, and Charlie might have been around to stop her.

As it turned out, Anne Sanderson had finally made a decision with results that worked out exactly as she had planned.

Over the course of several months, she had become more and more estranged from her husband, and though she had slapped Charlie when he suggested Brad was having an affair, she finally decided to find out for herself. It quickly became an obsession, and while her son Charlie was following around an electronic troll waiting for just the right moment to begin a relationship, so was his mother shadowing a real one, looking for the proper moment to end her own.

Had either Charlie or his mother known of the other's fixation, chances are that much subsequent tragedy would have been avoided, but such was not the case. As Charlie fixated on the personality known as **unwanted_image**, his mother became more and more determined to catch her husband in the act of adultery, so much so that it was almost all that she thought about. She *knew* he was cheating, but she had to *know*.

As a child, Anne's maternal grandfather, who would eventually grow up to marry a woman with an anxiety disorder, had been told by a friend that there was treasure inside the bricked over fireplace in the one-room school house they both attended. The boy thought of the treasure so often that he came to accept the reality of its existence and focused instead on how to retrieve it. He *knew* it was there, and he had to *get it*.

So he was shocked when he worked all day one Saturday chipping away at the mortar around a single, loose-looking brick, and when finally pulling it free, reached his arm as far as it would go into the void and feeling nothing in the dark but dust.

He had tricked his mind into accepting a fantasy as reality, and so had difficulty when the time came to perceive things as they really were.

Anne, of course, had the opposite problem. She had tricked her mind into believing a fantasy that she knew wasn't real, and it was oh, so easy to revert to reality. Dangerously easy. But she couldn't catch him in the act. He wore plausible deniability around his shoulders like some evil cloak of invincibility, urging her to take another pill and give up her paranoid delusions, all the while purposely feeding them to toy with her emotions, which only depressed her more.

When Charlie told his mother not to wait up, that he was going to see a girl, the conversation that might have passed between them as casual information even a week before turned into something more.

"What's her name?" she asked, and Charlie, who might have once reacted sullenly because of their fight, stopped to tell his mother all about Sarah, leaving out some parts, of course, such as where they'd met. It was the first substantial conversation they'd had in weeks, and they were like parched Bedouins in the desert. It was almost as if they had lost nothing of their relationship, but then the conversation turned, and it was as if the easy words had been a mirage.

"You were right, Charlie," his mother suddenly said.

"About what?"

"Brad. I know he's cheating."

Charlie's brow furrowed, his eyes dark. Brad had always been a sore spot between them, and the last time his name had been spoken it had been ugly.

"What are you doing with him, Mom?" Charlie nearly cried. Years of emotion poured out of him, all of the anger and bitterness about the betrayal of his father's memory and their ruined lives flowed forth like a nasty, poison river.

Anne just stood there and let it wash over her; she was almost happy for him to finally let it out. She should have been more open to it before.

When Charlie was done, he felt tired and empty, and his mother took him in her arms and held him, whispering over and over in his ear, "I'll make things right, son. I'll make things right."

When Charlie finally pulled away, his mother's eyes were peaceful for the first time in a very long time. He even thought he saw a glimmer of hope in there, somewhere. She wasn't happy, but she was, how could he describe it? *Reconciled.*

"You enjoy your time with Sarah, son," his mother said. "Life is short." And she smiled so sweetly that Charlie felt tears welling up in his eyes. He had been such an asshole to have stayed mad at her for so long. He could see that now. Everything seemed clear to him, now.

"I've gotta go, Mom," he said. "It's a long drive."

She nodded. "Yes. It's getting late."

Something bothered him about the way she said that, and it wasn't, of course, the fact that they were the very last words he ever heard his mother say. He had no idea of that at the time. It was the way she said it, with an almost dream-like quality. As if she had not actually accepted reality, but rather stepped into a fantasy, a world in which everything would be all right.

And both of them knew that just wasn't true.

Charlie made the three and a half hour drive in three, and he and Sarah were halfway through their meal when his mother sent him a text just before stepping off the vanity stool in her bedroom, swinging just a bit before the kicking stopped.

As soon as Charlie left, Anne had driven to her husband's office and finally caught her husband in the act, laughing and kissing his secretary as they left for the evening, probably to some fancy hotel downtown.

*She doesn't look like the cheap motel type,* Anne thought, giggling at her insight.

She entered the building after they'd left, and used the key to her husband's office she had managed to keep from him, despite all of his precautions. There were several of his employees there, and she smiled and greeted them each by name, explaining that her husband had forgotten some papers and asked her to stop by.

They knew she was lying, of course, but were too embarrassed to say anything at all. Their boss had just left with the woman they all knew to be his mistress; whatever else happened, it was none of their concern.

Anne went through his files and found what she was looking for, and used the series of neatly typed numbers to open the safe that was hidden in the floor beneath his desk. In spite of her generally drugged state, there was something purifying about her decision. Something that cleared her mind a bit. She hadn't really known whether she could do it until her conversation with Charlie, but somehow she knew he would be all right.

She gathered the documents from the safe and shredded them, making sure to take the fragments with her for disposal at some out-of-the-way location on her way home. She wasn't sure, but knowing Brad, he had kept all the copies in the safe for himself.

Just before she hung herself, she sent a text to Charlie. Had she been thinking clearly, she would have never done such a thing, or at least left him a note, but the clarity of their last conversation had, by this time, receded back into the depths of her psychosis, and it all made perfect sense to her.

Of course, had she been thinking clearly, she never would have taken her life at all, but as Charlie and his new friend understood better than most from the websites they frequented, almost anyone was capable of taking a life if the circumstances were right.

Her sordid family history never even crossed her mind, her childhood obsessions now long forgotten. Little did she know those same fascinations had already been transferred to her son.

***

When Charlie got the text, he knew immediately what it meant. Knowing his mother as he did, there was really no other explanation.

He looked up from his phone on the table and into Sarah's eyes, and his own were filled with terror.

"I have to go," Charlie said, and Sarah could find no words to respond. She had never seen such a look on the face of another human being, and she never wanted to again. She watched in silence as Charlie ran out of the restaurant, honestly not knowing if she would ever see him again.

And then she looked down and saw his phone, where the last words of his mother lay coiled like a snake in the sun, ready to rise up and strike whoever wandered past.

**I made things right. Love, Mom.**

The following 60 Minutes script is from "Judge Not".

Steve Kroft is the correspondent.

Samuel Grayson, Michael Dill, and Ariana Ortiz, producers.

*You wouldn't know it from his recent actions, but this Cook County,*

*Illinois criminal court judge, pictured on the left,*

[Graphic]

*was a man so well respected by his peers that he was nominated*

*numerous times, and recently won, The William H. Rehnquist Award*

*for Judicial Excellence, one of the highest honors in his profession.*

*This is the story behind the incredible events surrounding the trial of*

*mass school shooter Nathan Jackson, and how one judge ended both*

*his life and his exemplary career in a single, stunning moment that*

*will likely forever change the face of American jurisprudence.*

*Only last month, we reported on the growing TOWY movement, so*

*named as an acronym for "take one with you," which encourages those who plan suicide to literally take someone else with them to*

*their death. Towys, as they call themselves, want to kill someone else*

*before killing themselves. Preferably someone that society, or more*

*likely, the shadowy leaders of the movement, deems worthy.*

*Murderers, rapists, and child molesters initially topped the list.*

*But gradually, whether by design or because grass roots movements*

*by nature are unpredictable, the list of those deemed worthy,*

*expanded.*

*Nancy Janes, who clerked for Judge Spencer Wetherbee and*

*witnessed the event, recently sat for an interview.*

*Steve Kroft: What was it like working for Judge Wetherbee?*

*Nancy Janes: He was the best, just the best. I still can't believe he*

*actually did it.*

*Steve Kroft: What do you mean 'actually'?*

*Nancy Janes: Well, he kind of mentioned it before. Alluded, I guess.*

*Steve Kroft: How do you mean?*

*Nancy Janes: The case was all everybody was talking about, of*

*course, and he –*

*Steve Kroft: The Nathan Jackson case?*

*Nancy Janes: Yes. Judge Wetherbee just seemed really tired of it all.*

*Steve Kroft: Meaning?*

*Nancy Janes: The whole media circus. There was a lot of, um, pressure.*

*Steve Kroft: Go on.*

*Nancy Janes: Well, he was sick of it. He'd handled, oh God, so many criminal cases. But this was different. This one hit him hard.*

*Steve Kroft: You mean the children.*

*Nancy Janes: He has – had, grandchildren that age. And when he had to make that ruling, it broke his heart.*

*She's talking about a pre-trial defense motion to disallow the seizure of a laptop computer found at Nathan Jackson's mother's house that may have held evidence showing premeditation.*

*According to Nancy, Judge Wetherbee made statements to her that he was worried about the lack of such evidence and how it might affect the jury.*

*Nancy Janes: He was worried they might not convict on first degree and bump him down to second.*

*Steve Kroft: But how could that happen?*

*Nancy Janes: We don't have the death penalty. And when you've been a judge as long as he had, really…I mean, anything can happen.*

*Steve Kroft: These were children.*

*Nancy Janes: I guess that's why he wanted to make sure.*

*Illinois abolished the death penalty in 2011, and if the shooter had been convicted of second-degree murder, he could have been released in as few as four years.*

*Dr. Scott Robbins is a professor of criminal justice at Illinois State University. He also has degrees in sociology and clinical psychology.*

*Scott Robbins: Oh, it's quite possible that the shooter could have been convicted of the lesser charge. As terrible as it sounds, things like that happen all the time.*

*Steve Kroft: For shooting nine six year-olds, killing four of them?*

*Scott Robbins: It wasn't his gun. At least, they couldn't prove that it was. He could have found it on the way to the school, even at the scene, and just decided to shoot. Spur of the moment.*

*Steve Kroft: Spur of the moment?*

*Scott Robbins: This is Cook County.*

*Steve Kroft: Come on.*

*Scott Robbins: Look, if they'd been able to trace the gun, that might have made a difference. To show how or when he acquired it. But they couldn't. The previous owner could be out there somewhere, scared to death to be connected to the shooting, or blissfully unaware their gun is missing. Or dead. Who knows? There are a lot of unregistered, unlicensed guns out there. But unless they could prove when or where he got the gun, they couldn't necessarily prove premeditation.*

*Steve Kroft: Unless they had the laptop.*

*Scott Robbins: Unless they had the laptop.*

*Which brings us back to that ruling. Judge Wetherbee, by all accounts, was a stickler for the law. So when the police acquired the laptop outside the rules of evidence, the judge felt he had no choice but to exclude it.*

*Nancy Janes: Oh, it tore him up. Absolutely.*

*Steve Kroft: And that's when the pressure got to him?*

*Nancy Janes: I think so. He just couldn't stand the thought of that man not being punished for what he'd done.*

*Steve Kroft: But he still would have served time.*

*Nancy Janes: What time? Four years?*

*Steve Kroft: Second-degree murder is four to fifteen. And there was still a chance he could have been convicted of first-degree murder, wasn't there?*

*Nancy Janes: Maybe.*

*Steve Kroft: That could be life without parole.*

*Nancy Janes: But would that have been enough? Could it ever be enough, for what he did?*

*Apparently, Judge Wetherbee didn't think so. Because on the first*

*day of the trial, he smuggled into his chambers an antique Colt*

*Single Action Army .45 Revolver,*

[Graphic]

*also known, ironically enough, as a Peacemaker, first used during*

*the American-Indian Wars of the nineteenth century. Though its*

*cylinder holds six rounds, the weapon was loaded with only two.*


*Steve Kroft: Why do you think he did that?*

*Scott Robbins: Just two bullets? I guess he figured he was a pretty*

*good shot. Or else he was getting forgetful.*

*What Dr. Robbins is referring to are rumors of the judge's senility,*

*which have been refuted by his doctors, his family, and his friends.*

*None of Judge Wetherbee' relatives wanted to be interviewed on*

*camera, but a spokesperson for the family released a statement that*

*reads in part: "As for the number of bullets, we have no idea why he*

*chose to load the number he did, except that which is obvious to*

*those who knew him: Judge Wetherbee wanted to hurt only two people, the accused and himself, and that was his way of ensuring*

*it."*

*There were no other weapons or ammunition found anywhere in the*

*judge's chambers, his home, or his car.*

*When we return, video of the event itself, up until the moment he*

*pulled the trigger.*

[Commercial break]

*What you're about to see is the extraordinary footage from the first*

*day of the trial of school shooter Nathan Jackson, Judge Spencer*

*Wetherbee presiding. We won't show the actual shooting, but please*

*be advised the content may be disturbing to some viewers.*

[Video]

*As you can see, the judge has ordered the armed bailiffs to stand to*

*each side of the bench, facing out towards the courtroom. This was*

*unusual, but most onlookers probably assumed, after his next*

*direction, that it was for his own protection.*

*They assumed wrong.*

*Judge Wetherbee: Before we bring in the jury, I'd like to say a few things. Mr. Dalworth, would you instruct your client to stand and approach the bench, please?*

*As you can see, the defense attorney brings Nathan Jackson forward, but then the judge surprises everyone for the second time.*

*Judge Wetherbee: You can sit down, Counsel.*

*Mr. Dalworth: Your honor?*

*Judge Wetherbee: Please take a seat. Thank you. Mr. Jackson, you have been incarcerated for some time, now. Your meals, your protection, and your care are all paid for by Cook County. You were brought here under armed guard wearing a bulletproof vest, walking amongst men who are trained to step in the way of an assassin in order to protect your life, all so that you may be tried in a court of law by a jury of your peers. Your trial, and many others like it, along with the probable appeals, will inevitably take many months, if not years, to conclude. It is, in my view, a colossal waste of the State's resources.*

*Mr. Dalworth: Your honor –*

*Judge Wetherbee: Sit down, Mr. Dalworth. You'll have your chance to speak in a moment. My point, Mr. Jackson, is that an awful lot of time and money will be spent on you, and the media will endlessly blather on and on and your name will become commonly known and possibly even glorified, and it will be like many other trials I've witnessed in my thirty years on this bench. A lot of sound and fury, signifying nothing but pain for your victims, this community, and society at large.*

*Mr. Dalworth: Your honor!*

*Judge Wetherbee: Sit down, Mr. Dalworth! Do you know what I mean, Mr. Jackson? That's from Macbeth, act five, by the way. The full quote is, "A tale told by an idiot, full of sound and fury, signifying nothing." Mr. Jackson, I am that idiot. As well as my peers, and society in general. For continuously allowing our judicial system to be perverted by the likes of you. Stay in your seat, Mr. Dalworth, and you can ask for a mistrial. Mr. Jackson, I've decided to stop being an idiot. I find you guilty as hell!*

*We've frozen the tape there, but at that point, Judge Wetherbee drew his weapon from beneath his robe, stood up, and before a shocked courtroom, shot Nathan Jackson between the eyes. He then turned*

*the weapon on himself. Both men died instantly.*


*We may never know what motivated Judge Wetherbee, after a life*

*devoted to serving the law as a judge, to appoint himself jury and*

*executioner, as well. But we do know this: There are an awful lot of*

*so-called Towys out there who had vowed to do exactly the same*

*thing to Nathan Jackson if ever they got the opportunity.*

*Judge Wetherbee, because he'd had enough, denied them that*

*chance.*

# **Chapter Seven**

"I could cut your throat like a chicken and nobody would give a fuck."

The larger of the two men in the alley silently appraised his adversary through slitted, almost feral eyes, breathing heavily. Both men knew the words reflected a hard truth in an even harder city, the kind of truth that wasn't so much conscious knowledge as it was something deeper, almost like a gene passed down from father to son.

There were a lot of people in the city who wouldn't be missed should something tragic befall them, people who looked like they'd already fallen through the cracks a few times before and somehow managed, against all odds, to crawl back into the light to await a similar fate.

People like the man being pushed up against the wall with a knife to his throat.

What the speaker of those words had no way of knowing was that the object of his derision, though a derelict through and through, was not one of those people.

The smaller man, the one holding a knife to the big man's throat, the speaker of those cold, hard words, pressed the blade a little deeper into the larger man's flesh, an especially nasty glint in his eye.

"You know what I mean, you piece of shit?"

The bigger man nodded once, being careful not to move much at all given the sharp steel against his skin. It was really more of a look in his eyes than a movement of his head, but he sensed the smaller man wanted something more. He was already bleeding from several places after the beating he'd taken, and had no desire at all to test the sincerity of the smaller man's claim, especially when it would be his own knife that would be cutting his throat.

"Lemme hear you say it," the man with the knife hissed, pressing harder. The big man could feel his life pulsing beneath metal, an odd thing to experience, indeed.

One summer when he was a boy he'd hiked through the woods with some buddies to an old dam during a drought, and after they'd snuck past two fences, one of them had dared him to walk across the cement shoulder to the other side. It was about the width of two shoes, not that hard to balance, but falling to either side would likely mean serious injury or death.

It was the longest 200 feet he'd ever traveled, and about halfway across the dam he got the same queasy feeling in the pit of his stomach that he felt now, in a darkened alley behind a liquor store just a block from the cheap flophouse where he always stayed until his check ran out, which was usually about the middle of each month.

Like his life was teetering on the edge of something cold and unfeeling, something that would just as soon have him die as live.

Just as it had always been. The larger of the two men had lived a precarious life for as long as he could remember, and the edge was all he knew. A blade, a concrete wall, a tripwire in Kandahar. It was somehow all the same. He felt his body relax, and he could see in the smaller man's eyes that he'd felt it, too.

"I said say it," the man with the knife repeated, and suddenly the larger man wanted desperately to live, a desire he hadn't felt in a very long time.

"I want to live," he croaked, and for a moment the man with the knife looked at him oddly, as if he were a particularly puzzling specimen he had pinned beneath his microscope, which was really not that far from the truth, in a way.

Then the smaller man laughed, and it was the laugh that landed the larger man in the hospital, and it was the laugh that probably saved his life.

It was an evil-sounding laugh, a contagious cackle that reminded the big man of everyone who had ever mocked him, from his lumpy, oversized childhood to basic training to his prison days, and it turned his emotions on a dime. He was right back to the semi-homeless derelict who'd ripped the plastic bag filled with chips and candy from the hands of a nine year-old boy, who was now cowering a few feet away and long forgotten by both men.

He was right back to being someone with nothing to lose.

The smaller man was taken completely by surprise when the larger man suddenly pushed off the wall, knocking the knife from his hand and causing him to fall backwards into a row of garbage bags piled next to an overflowing dumpster, and like the laugh that saved the big man's life, the garbage saved his own. He hit that pile of trash at the perfect angle to enable a quick draw of his duty weapon, and he pulled it out and fired just as the big man jumped.

***

"Jesus Christ, Thane."

Thane Parks, the man who'd seen the derelict rip off the kid at knifepoint after leaving the liquor store, shrugged his shoulders and smiled tiredly at his boss, the chief of detectives. Myers always showed up whenever one of his men discharged his weapon, even if it was inconsequential, which this was decidedly not.

Behind them, paramedics were loading the big man into the back of an ambulance.

"And where you're headed, holy shit."

Thane laughed, a slightly less evil-sounding version than what had set off the derelict, and his boss reluctantly joined in. "I know, I know." Thane looked past Myers where a female officer with a pretty decent rack was talking to the kid with the candy. He was divorced, his ex-wife was a bitch, and he definitely wouldn't mind tapping that ass before the ceremony.

But he also needed to talk with that kid. Thane had told the boy to go home before he dragged the big man into the alley, but somehow he'd either been too scared or too curious and apparently had seen and heard a little too much for the detective's taste.

Thane noticed the female officer didn't have her notebook out, which was good, but she'd be handing the kid off to social services soon, or maybe his parents if they were around, and that couldn't happen without a few words in private.

"Speaking of which, Lieutenant..." Thane said, and Myers nodded.

"Yeah, yeah, get the hell out of here," he said. "I'll see you there."

"Thanks," Thane said, and walked towards the kid as Myers went to talk to another officer who was taking notes by flashlight next to the pile of trash.

As he approached, the boy's eyes grew wide and the officer turned to see Thane. She stood up and for a moment Thane thought she was going to salute him or something.

*Rookie,* he thought. *Love to bang the newbies.*

Thane looked her up and down. She looked even better up close.

*Wedding ring. Fuck. On second thought, even better. No commitments.*

"Detective Parks?"

"Yeah, that's me," Thane said, his eyes rising to hers and then back down to her tightly packed tits. "Officer Hellstrom."

She flushed. It was clear she had thought he was staring at her chest and he'd sufficiently covered by pretending to search for her nametag.

"Yes, hi."

Thane smiled. "Hi."

There was a brief moment of silence as Thane just waited for her to speak. He liked the fact that she was slightly uncomfortable and off guard.

Thane Parks enjoyed watching people flounder.

Finally he put her out of her misery, but filed away her reaction for another time. He liked watching her flounder all right, but he'd really like to feel her wriggle.

"You mind if I have a word?" he asked, and nodded towards the boy, who was still staring up at him, eyes wide.

"Oh, sure," she said, stepping to the side. "Do you sign?"

For a moment, Thane thought she was asking for his star sign like they were in some 80's singles bar, and then he realized that she meant the kid was deaf.

*Now that is fucking beautiful. The only thing better would be if-*

"He can't speak, either," the officer said.

Thane was about to upbraid her about assumptions since the kid might be in shock, but gently, so as not to ruin his chance for a future piece of ass, when he noticed that the kid was holding one of those cards that deaf mutes hand out for donations. He'd caught one or two scammers with those cards before, but this kid looked a little too young for that.

*Looks like my lucky day.*

He reached down to touch the kid's shoulder, but the boy cowered behind the female officer, wrapping his arms around her waste.

*Kid may be dumb, but he's no dummy.*

Thane smiled as warmly as he could at the kid, and ran his eyes back up Officer Goodbody's good body. "Poor little guy's seen a lot, tonight," he said, and received a smile from Hellstrom. "I guess he's in good hands."

"Waiting for social services," she said.

Thane looked at his watch, which wasn't working, more as a segue to leaving than actually checking the time. He never wore a working watch, and if by some miracle one of his watches actually started working, he'd either take out the battery or throw it out. "Well, I really gotta take off."

"I heard," she said. "Congratulations."

He was surprised. "Oh, yeah? Thanks. Thanks a lot."

Thane started to turn away and decided to go for it. *No better time than the present,* thought the man who refused to wear a working timepiece.

"When does your shift end, Hellstrom?" he asked. "I wouldn't mind taking a date to the dinner."

She blushed again, which pleased Thane greatly, but then he saw her arm moving and knew she was about to hold up her ring finger as a way to refuse his invitation, and decided to beat her to the punch.

"Oh, Jesus, you're married," he said apologetically. "I didn't mean anything by it, you know. I'm divorced, it's kind of a thing – "

"No, that's okay," she said, a little too quickly, and Thane knew she was a possible future fuck. He was a damn good detective, a student of human nature, and cops were notoriously an unhappy and therefore, unfaithful, bunch of misfits. He gave himself a forty percent chance of getting into what he imagined were some tight little panties if he worked it right, especially if her husband was a civilian. Forty-five if he was a cop.

"My husband's on the desk at Hill Street," she said, "it would have been fun to tell him about it, but I'm on till one."

Thane grinned a little too wolfishly, but he was feeling pretty good. *Forty-five, fifty,* he thought. "No problem," he said. "Next time."

She blushed again. *Make a terrible poker player, but a real nice poke.*

"Sure," she said.

Thane turned and walked towards his car, which was still parked in front of the liquor store. He knew better than to look back. *Let her watch me and wonder. Marvel at the glorious majesty of my detective status!*

He laughed. Only a beat cop would be impressed with his status, actually. Thane was a damn good detective but a lousy politician, and his rise within the department had been stifled more than once by his stubborn refusal to kiss the right ass at the proper time.

He was also a good father, but his ex-wife and his department had seen to it that his advancement within those realms would never be what he wanted them to be. The job he could have taken in stride, but the way his ex used his kid against him had turned him into a bitter man.

A bitter man with a gun.

Thane suffered from bouts of depression as a result, although he would not have understood it as such. He drank too much and gambled too much to cope with the fact that his ex did everything in her power to deny him access to his child, which she in turn used against him to further limit his visitations. She had an asshole dyke of an attorney who hated cops, at least that was what he chose to believe, and he was often forced to petition the court for privileges he imagined a typical divorced father would routinely be granted without such action.

So he drank even more and spent time with loose women and tight slot machines, which only made things worse.

But he'd never missed a support payment and he never would, not as long as he drew breath. One day he'd be vindicated and his son would know what an evil bitch their mother was and how much he'd sacrificed for him.

One day.

But not today.

He drove straight to the hotel, his mind replaying the events of the evening. He'd been on his way home after a long day, eager for a hot shower and a nap before the big show, and he'd stopped for a pint he figured to knock back before the party to take the edge off what he knew was coming. All those pricks he was going to see.

When he saw the kid walk out of the store with that bag of candy, he was reminded of his own son, who was about that age. Christ, he was missing so many moments of his life because of that cunt!

The big guy had come out of nowhere and just snatched the bag, the glint of his knife flashing beneath the streetlight on the corner.

Thane was so shocked he almost let the guy get away, but it was that flash of steel that woke him up. The guy was huge, probably 6'5" and 260, and even though he didn't threaten the kid with the knife, the thought that he had it in his hand when he grabbed the bag, filled Thane with blind rage.

He jumped out of his car, told the kid to get lost, and set out to beat the man to death. He wanted to ruin his fists on the son-of-a-bitch.

Only it didn't happen quite the way he expected. Thane was smaller, but he was still a pretty big guy, a former boxer as a teen, but this asshole had skills. Some kind of martial arts, and Thane got lucky with the knife, turning it on its owner.

Some of the hate had drained out of him, by that time, but he was still on the edge of slicing the guy's throat, and told him so.

Except for the kid. The kid was watching.

Thane turned it over in his mind all the way to the hotel, unsure of whether he would have actually killed the guy.

He was wearing dog tags and had tattoos that indicated he'd served in the military, so maybe he was fucked up with PTSD or something. Thane wasn't concerned with all that, though. In an odd way, he understood that he was filled with rage and that he had developed a dangerous habit of taking it out on those he arrested, but he didn't care.

God help him, he didn't care.

As far as he was concerned, there were too goddamn many scumbags in the world, and if he could help get rid of a few of them, well, what the hell was wrong with that?

When he rose from his seat at the dinner to receive his award for "innovative community policing", an award that would never, ever lead to the position within the department he deserved, he looked out into the faces of the brass that had continually passed him over for promotions over the years, and thought of what a service it would be to take a few of them out, as well.

As he sat down to what he considered restrained applause, he thought of Officer Hellstrom and wondered how he could maneuver himself between her legs at his earliest convenience.

Innovative community policing always made him horny.

At that very moment, Officer Hellstrom was thinking of him, too.

Just as he had assumed at the scene, she had indeed watched him walk away, all the way back to his car. Then she'd turned back to the boy, indicating to him that he could continue telling her his story in ASL, otherwise known as American Sign Language.

After that, Detective Thane Parks was very much on her mind.

# 3 MONTHS AFTER TOWY WEBSITE

Reddit, if you had a
daughter who was gang
raped, would you kill the
pricks? (self.AskReddit)
submitted 3 minutes ago by kola24y
**134 comments**
**share**
all 134 comments
sorted by:
**new**
[–]**Z0omboy** 1 minute ago
Death. Nothing else need be said. Your talking Turner 3,
right? Didnt scroll.

    **permalink**[–]**heruskael** 1 minute agoHoly shit. TOWY got
them.


    **permalinkparent**[–]**bitatch** 1 minute agotwo girls even
threatening her. those people are shit, i could not even believe
anyone would even think to harass their rape victm, much less
for a fucking year. got what they deserved. Towy is fukn
awesome

    **permalink**
    **parent**
[–]**rambler** 1 minute ago
murder is impossible for rapists. not murder i m4an. Lol fuck
cant type. murder always justified for rape.

  **permalink**[–]**Wawesome** 1 minute agoI have a daughter. I
would be on trial for wwhen I found out.

    **permalink**   [–]**Llaster** 1 minute agojustifiable homo-side.
**permalink**
**parent**
[–]**HadoBlade** 1 minute ago
turner 3. The hockey players that raped that chick. Fuck em.
Towy set 'em up and knocked 'em down.

**permalink[–]Not4ENT** 2 minutes agoMiserable fucks. She had to quit school. Went psycho. Offed herself. dad found her in a tub fulla blood. Jesus fucking Christ. Not gonna find any votes for those a-holes. TOWY RAWKS!! Take one with you. Hell, take two or three, like the Turner 3!

**permalink[–]Byayah** 2 minutes agoTerminator style. Wonder who offed them? I heard they couldn't prosecutr cause she never told anyone at the time.

**permalink　[–]suriisdumb** 2 minutes agoNuke the whole high school. only way to be sure.

**permalink[–]mixologist2145**[S] 2 minutes agoreminds me of stubnville.

**permalink　　[–]bewellll** 2 minutes agosomebody hacked their shit n posted it on that towy cite.

**permalink[–]Digitaldoctor** 3 minutes agoThey should be doing minimum 1000 years gettn raped themselves.

**permalink**

# Chapter Eight

Charlie refused to communicate with Sarah for several months after the death of his mother, even though they still frequented the same message boards. He knew she was stalking him online, though, and took a perverse pleasure in ignoring her presence in threads he started with increasing frequency, musing about things to people who were not at all the type of people with whom he would normally discuss such things.

One of the poor depressed souls Charlie began to communicate with more often was `clairebear`, who was extremely depressed about the death of her sister. Charlie had introduced `clairebear` and Sarah online a few months before, which was one of the reasons Charlie took a renewed interest in her.

`clairebear` wouldn't give many details about her depression except that her sister had been murdered and she had been considering suicide ever since. Sarah had taken a hard line position with her on the message boards, annoying others who were much less direct and more openly compassionate, but that had always been Sarah's style. She definitely leaned towards tough love as opposed to a sympathetic ear.

Charlie refused to tell `clairebear` exactly what had happened between himself and Sarah that led to their break, but perhaps because he had always been the "good cop" in his and Sarah's unofficial online intervention, it was Charlie to whom the depressed girl gravitated.

`clairebear` interacted less and less with Sarah and sought out Charlie more and more, in private, direct communications outside the message boards she frequented before. Charlie and the girl grew closer emotionally, but he thought there was something inside her that was dead and irretrievably broken.

Charlie had no doubt that some day **clairebear** would simply disappear, failing to respond to messages or frequent the boards, and then he would know that she had finally gathered the courage to end her life.

Since he'd found his mother hanging from a beam in the master bedroom, Charlie's views on the bravery of suicides had changed drastically. There was a time after his father died when Charlie had contemplated harming himself. The feeling grew strongest when he felt he was losing his mother to his stepfather, which was why he was searching out other depressed people in the first place.

He wasn't quite aware of it at that time, but he eventually understood he was looking for validation. Permission to take his own life.

But he never found it.

Even to those sympathetic to the darker forces of human nature and privy to the pain so many suffered, suicide was still considered a cowardly act.

It wasn't described in such stark terms by most of the people with whom he interacted, of course, but there was always an undercurrent that it was "the easy way out," an opinion Charlie himself shared.

Until the death of his mother.

To think of his mother as weak was something that often crossed Charlie's mind when she was alive; to be sure, it was the cause of much of the conflict that persisted between them after she remarried. Charlie was a smart kid, but he was still a kid, and he had the typical teenage mentality that he knew more than the adults who raised him.

But after her death, he began to think more seriously about the sacrifices his mother made for him, which included marrying a man like Brad because she wanted to make sure her son was taken care of, and staying with him in spite of his cheating and mental abuse for the same reason.

In his mind, Charlie's mother was a hero, and heroes did not act in a cowardly fashion.

Charlie couldn't even consider her demise self-inflicted. For a time he described it as an assisted suicide, but that gave Brad too much credit. Assistance sounded like there was something positive in what he'd done.

So Charlie settled on murder.

As far as he was concerned, his stepfather had murdered his mother.

And that was how the seeds of TOWY began to form in his mind. Out of grief and anger and his own warped sense of his mother, who, like most parents, was neither saint nor sinner, just a woman who tried to do her best for her child. Even her prescription drug abuse became, in the mind of her son, an act of nobility.

The worldwide TOWY movement began because Charlie fervently wished that his mother had thought of one more thing, one more heroic act, to take his stepfather with her.

Sometimes he dreamed of the day his mother died. In his dreams, Charlie wasn't stopped for speeding mere minutes from his house. He wasn't held up for those crucial moments. In this dream, he always arrived just as she stepped off the stool, and he would rush in to catch her. She would cry and hug him, and then Charlie would cut her down with a knife that always seemed to appear in his hand, and the two of them would leave the house and never return.

It was a nice dream, a sweet dream, but he never felt satisfied when he woke up. There was no residual good feeling at all, even for a moment. Not because he knew it wasn't real, but because it did not satisfy his need for revenge.

The dream that haunted his thoughts was a dream that he *wanted to have*. A dream he laid awake at night imagining in the hopes he could will it into being.

In this dream his mother did not live, however. In this dream his mother still committed suicide, but first she killed her husband.

She took Brad with her.

It was a dream that Charlie so desperately wanted to experience, even once, but which never came. Since his mother would still be dead when he awoke, Charlie saw no need for a nice dream to mock his reality. He preferred a nasty, darker dream, something that could give him a taste of what he needed.

Something that would give him the courage to kill Brad.

That was the real reason he never breached the wall he'd built between himself and Sarah after his mother's death. Sure, he had blamed her for insisting they meet that fateful night, but his anger at Sarah had faded within hours. He knew his mother would have just chosen another day when he wasn't home. After all, it only took minutes for her to die. She could have even killed herself when he was online in the next room and he never would have known until it was too late.

The real reason he cut off all communication from Sarah was because he knew she would talk him out of what he planned to do.

So `clairebear` became his confidant. He was still resentful of Sarah, but that was something, deep down, he knew was illogical. But he kept it alive to keep himself from contacting her. To stay focused. He needed the illusion to stoke the fires of revenge in his heart. He was like a blacksmith holding tongs in the fire, waiting for the right temperature so he could pound and shape the iron into his weapon of choice.

Charlie would never stop hating Brad, but he couldn't quite manage the strength to kill him, either. He was getting a taste of what had torn his mother apart, a feeling of helplessness.

Ironically, it was `clairebear`, a girl who had earlier seemed to him the epitome of weakness, of depression unfettered by will, who both gave Charlie the courage to kill and prevented him from using it.

She also brought Charlie and Sarah back together, in a way. `clairebear` and the one who would come to be called the Pioneer did.

***

JT discovered completely by accident that the little old man he knew as Mister Tee, short for Mister Thomas, was actually Rodrigo Umberto Espinosa, also known as El Culo de Arica, also known as the Asshole of Arica. And even if he had known, JT probably would not have had the strength to do what he did, except for a transcontinental phone call that the old man himself had insisted on.

Each morning, Mister Tee was waiting when JT unlocked the doors to the pool room, which was actually more of an enormous lanai that covered the Olympic-style lap pool in which the old man swam.

On the one morning that he was late unlocking the pool, Mister Tee took notice, and JT told him the reason had been a call from the tiny hospital in Spain where his maternal grandmother lived. Her health had taken a turn and JT had spoken only with her caregiver, but the old man wanted to hear all about it.

JT, who had a good relationship with everyone at the club and looked at the older members almost like family elders, was eager to share. He had only recently reconnected with his grandmother, an early widow who'd left for Europe with a wealthy suitor many years before the death of her only daughter, JT's mother.

JT had discovered his illness about a year before they reconnected, and his symptoms had rapidly worsened. He'd gone through months of panic attacks and irrational fears, dealing with sleepless, sweaty nights with the alarm clock his only salvation.

Recently he'd been hallucinating quite a bit, which made him think more and more of his father and the stories he'd told of his grandfather, who had died with the reputation of mental illness instead of the sickness which had finally overtaken him.

JT could only imagine what it must have been like for someone who went through such turmoil without a diagnosis, as his grandfather did. He also gained new respect for his father, who was spared the genetic malady, but would be waylaid by a much more common enemy of their people, alcohol. As far back as he could remember, his father had been described as a crazy drunk, even by his own relatives, but his old man had always been steadfast in his defense of his father.

"He warn't crazy, son," his dad would say, "just bad spirits," which JT always thought was his dad's way of saying that JT's grandfather was also fond of the bottle, but hadn't been so sure.

More and more, JT had seen spirits in the night, hallucinations like the ones he imagined had tormented his grandfather. He dreaded that he would be completely overtaken by them.

JT didn't want to see anything like that in the light of day.

One night he was visited by the spirit brothers Iktomi and Iya, the shape-shifting trickster and his younger sibling, whose stories JT had heard as a boy.

"Jesus," Iktomi screeched, "Jesus Two Bears!"

The spirit spread out his arms, which became eight, and his little brother Iya appeared from his loins and sliced a razor-thin finger lengthwise along the flesh of each of his brother's limbs, releasing the bloody veins like flags unfurled on a windy day.

At the end of each vein was a tiny version of JT, hanging from a noose and laughing and dancing like a crazed marionette. Blood flowed from each tiny eye, which Iya happily sucked through a straw.

JT tried to scream himself awake, but he was not sleeping. He simply had to endure this and other hallucinations as a prisoner of his rapidly deteriorating mind.

Soon he would sleep less and less, eventually remaining awake for weeks or even months, after which the final stage would deliver dementia and death to his doorstep.

Faced with his mortality, he had been thinking more and more of ending his life. JT had no family left that he knew of besides his maternal grandmother, and he had not seen her for many years, not even when his mother died. He was well-liked by the members of the country club, but he had been a drifter for years and so had a loner's mentality, acquiring not so much friends as many useful acquaintances.

JT had no allusions that he would be missed, but the thought of descending into madness as his grandfather had done bothered him a great deal.

He found suicide a complicated issue, however. Historically the Native community had a high rate of suicide that the elders believed were tied to the historic loss of lands and the slow erosion of their heritage and traditions, and which the younger generation saw as poverty on the reservations and the resulting lack of opportunity. JT had always been proud of the fact that he had risen above his circumstances, and his mother, in particular, had always encouraged him not to be bound by such things. He knew the idea of suicide would disappoint her spirit, and leave his to walk the earth wailing until the date of his natural death arrived.

At least that was what his mother believed.

After her death, his father's friends held a ceremony to wipe away the tears, as they had for his dad, followed by a good sweat, during which Jesus' dad had seen his first vision in the small wood and rock structure buried halfway below ground.

He saw the face of his father across the steaming rocks. Once again, he told his son the story of his grandfather's bravery at Wounded Knee.

As he reached the climax of the tale, his father's face morphed into that of Iktomi, who repeated the words his father had so often used as both admonishment and encouragement. "Take your stand, boy," he said. "Look it in the eye, and take your stand."

"It", of course, had been the 7th Cavalry to his ancestors at Wounded Knee, the U.S. Marshals to his grandfather at the same location, and the bottle to his father, wherever he happened to be at the time.

Evil was many things to many people.

But Jesus Two Bears could not bring himself to do it, if 'it' referred to suicide. He could not dishonor the memory of his parents and grandparents in such a way.

And that was how he came to search for his grandmother, an old woman with Alzheimer's living in a tiny hospital-clinic in Spain, who would eventually lead the entire world to the Asshole of Arica.

# 1 MONTH AFTER TOWY WEBSITE

**Fax**

To: DET. THANE PARKS          From: S. HARRISON

Fax: ▮▮▮▮▮▮▮▮          Pages:

Phone:          Date:

Re: ACCIDENT RPT. 57652-13          CC:

WILLIAMSON, MELISSA

☐ Comment  ☒ Review  ☐ Reply  ☐ Urgent    ✳ DO NOT REDISTRIBUTE

● Comments: ATTACHED AS PER REQUEST. CORONERS PIC FROM SCENE. NOTE- LEFT PORTION OF TATTOO MISSING DUE TO AVULSION TRAUMA. HIGHER RES UNAVAILABLE. BUT CAN SEND COLOR IF NEEDED.

# **<u>Chapter Nine</u>**

Melissa thought both of them were acting like children.

She had met Charlie first and then Sarah, although "met" was always a weird way to describe any online relationship, at least the way she conducted them.

It was always one way or no way.

If she had thought about it on a conscious level, she might have realized that she was looking for another Claire, someone to tell her exactly what to do at exactly the right time, but as it was, no one ever got enough information out of her to even begin to address what was bothering her. She would never again let anyone close to her.

Melissa was like a sponge that never dried up or allowed evaporation, sucking up the pain of others but never releasing her own. She just wanted it all to be over. In the river of life, she was treading water as she floated downstream, praying her limbs would give out and she would find blessed release.

But she found something, a bit of hope, maybe, in Charlie.

Both of them knew that she had lost a sister, but the details were never divulged outside of her being murdered. It was as if the tiny part of Claire that still lived inside her was too fragile to be exposed even for a moment, lest she be lost in the wind like a statue made of dust.

And because no details were offered, all advice and counsel was rendered meaningless platitudes, which were Melissa's only comfort.

She had constructed for herself a fortress of pain, and ironically, she needed help maintaining her isolation. Charlie and Sarah provided that. Anything more was anathema to the memory of her sister. So she used them, used their obvious compassion, to assist in her self-imposed confinement.

Had she not had their contact, Melissa knew she would go mad from the depression, and madness would not allow her to feel the agony she needed to experience.

The pain she *deserved*.

When she and her sister were young, waiting for a family who would accept both of them into their home, Claire and Melissa would play a little game. They would sit at whatever window was available at whatever time it was free of prying eyes, and they would wait for their Bandit.

Bandit had been a puppy owned by the cook at the group home they were sent to immediately following the death of their parents. He was such a happy little dog that the woman began to bring him to work with her, in the hopes it might cheer up the two new girls, who were frightened and inconsolable.

The cook would arrive at the home every day six o'clock on the dot, and little Bandit would tumble out of her old beater station wagon and onto the gravel driveway, following her into the kitchen. The other children there were singles, and the young ones went to families fast. The older ones were generally sullen and angry and uninterested in the cook and her little rat dog, and so Claire and Melissa had the pup mostly to themselves.

They would wake up early every morning to wait for the sight of that dog, play with it as much as they were allowed between chores and lessons, and then watch again in the evening when it would follow its owner out the door at six.

Once they left the home for their first foster family, and throughout their time between and with others, whenever Melissa got depressed, Claire would make her sit by the window to wait for her Bandit, which might end up being anything from a shooting star to the mailman to the backfire of a neighbor's car.

Whatever it was, they would both know it, and then they would look at each other and giggle. Melissa caught on pretty quickly that it was just a game of concentration. If she was waiting for something to happen, eventually something would. And as she waited, whatever sadness she was feeling would dissipate, at least for a time.

Until the next Bandit.

Neither Sarah nor Charlie was her Bandit, but rather they served as her Claire, or at least a shadow of her sister. They were her reminder that a Bandit was coming, that a Bandit was always on its way, whether it was a shooting star or a mailman or the backfire of a car or a motorcycle, eventually her pain would be relieved.

Charlie and Sarah never knew until later that Melissa had been communicating with them both during their estrangement, though they might have assumed so. She had no inclination to be some kind of mediator; it was obvious they would end up together because they were so clearly in love.

Even online and in er stupor, she could discern that. But her interest was not in their personal lives. The truth was, she couldn't have cared less about their problems or their lives. All human feeling had died in her. With her sister.

Melissa was mostly just killing time until she found the guts to kill herself. Her online friend Charlie told her that one day, she would snap out of it. He assured her that she would experience something or meet someone who would change everything, although wishing his mother took Brad intrigued her, mostly.

And then she "met" Jesus Two Bears.

***

After speaking with his doctor, a very compassionate man to whom he was referred after several others had failed to diagnose his disease, JT was convinced to seek out his grandmother. In reality, his physician thought the search might help take his patient's mind off suicide, which he was clearly considering even though JT had not come right out and said so.

From what the doctor was told by JT, his grandmother had disappeared overseas years ago, and it might take him some time to find her. The doctor, an elderly man nearing his retirement, had a lot of experience over the course of his career with the terminally ill, and if there was one thing they all could use, it was time and something worthwhile to occupy it.

But JT had found her almost immediately. She was as crazy as a rabid bat and twice as irascible, but she remembered everything from thirty years ago as clear as if it happened yesterday.

JT was able to communicate with her via email, and spent hours writing long, involved missives to her, to which she would often respond with a single sentence which didn't reveal whether or not she'd understood a word he'd written, or even read it. He was sure that her caregiver was unenthusiastically responding on her behalf most times.

He wasn't even convinced that she understood who he was until he mentioned the story of his name, and then she replied with a message that was written in such a way that it might have been a transcript of his mother's version he had been so familiar with. It amazed him, and gave him some hope that she might understand who he actually was.

She became his quest, his reason to get up in the morning, his excuse to go on living even as he felt like he was slowly becoming as dotty as she was. She gradually warmed to him, although he still wasn't entirely sure how much she understood, and sometimes her caregiver would write to tell him she was doing poorly or unable to sit up at the computer. He would send her a little note each day, sometimes for weeks on end, until she would finally respond and then they would continue their electronic correspondence.

Sometimes it seemed to JT that as he declined, she became a little more lucid in their exchanges, but it may have been his mind playing tricks on him.

He called to speak to her only once but it went badly, and she didn't return his emails for weeks. He worried that the tenuous connection had been irreparably damaged, but then one day she emailed him with a sweet story about his mother, and their relationship continued.

It wasn't until he suddenly lost consciousness at the country club that he tried to call her again, goaded by El Culo de Arica.

***

JT had been feeling weaker lately, sleeping less and less, with his visions becoming more terrifying. The spirit brothers were arguing over him in these hallucinations, sometimes pulling him back and forth like a ghostly tug-of-war. Often he woke up the neighbors, none of whom knew his condition, and there was talk around the building he would be asked to leave his little studio apartment.

JT's only real solace came from his sporadic contact with his grandmother half a world away. She was almost literally keeping him alive.

Soon he would no longer be able to work. His duties at the club had been reduced to opening the pool at five every morning, even though there was only the one old man who showed up to swim at that hour.

He supposed Mister Tee was keeping him alive, too.

Not long before his seizure, he had had a particularly rough night with the brothers. Iktomi, the elder, had taken the form of his mother, something he had never done before, and she had berated him for his unaccomplished existence, something she never would have done in life.

JT arrived at the club twenty minutes late, something he had never done before.

Mister Tee was waiting.

"What's the matter, boy?" he said, not unkindly.

"I'm sorry, Mister Tee," JT answered. "Rough night."

"Has llegado algún gatito!" he said, his eyes lighting up.

JT had never once heard the old man speak Spanish, and laughed in spite of himself. The old man was congratulating him on getting some action, but in an oddly formal way.

"No, nothing like that, Mister Tee," he answered. "Just tired, I guess."

"Let me in," the old man commanded, and JT unlocked the door, but once inside, Mister Tee was eager to ask him all about what he still assumed was his successful conquest.

"No, really," JT said, and then he explained the actual reason for his fatigue, which seemed to interest the old man even more. He insisted JT tell him more about the evil spirits, which led to his disease, which led to his grandmother. The old man seemed to really respond to JT's troubles.

"Why don't you go see her?"

"No money," JT said. "And I'm not sure how she would react, with the Alzheimer's."

From that point on, Mister Tee and the person whose final breath he would soon witness became fast friends. Eventually the older man even began to delay his morning swim just so he could hear updates from JT and his strange hallucinations.

JT assumed what he and many others had always believed, that he was talking to a sweet old man who was genuinely interested because he was lonely, but nothing could have been further from the truth. El Culo de Arica had relied on such assumptions for many years and become very good at cultivating them, but he was still the same monster he'd been since he was a child, only wilier and slightly more patient with his prey.

Like Iktomi, the shape-shifting spirit who tormented JT's nights as different people but who always reverted to his original form, a spider, the old man remained, at his essence, a lover of suffering. He looked back on his younger days with fondness, his only regret that he wasn't able to enjoy his sadistic hobbies more completely.

Still, JT's stories about his mother and their lives reminded him of his own family, who he'd abandoned when he left Peru. He cared nothing for his wife, an ugly woman who'd been unable to bear him a son, but there was a single daughter, with child when he left, and though he'd always planned to send for them, he had never been able to do so. It was the single soft spot in the heart of a devil, and Jesus Two Bears had managed to find it with his simple goodness.

And so El Culo de Arica was careless.

People who commit crimes against humanity are never really safe; there is always someone, somewhere, looking for them. The Asshole was no different. But El Culo had been able to avoid detection for so many years not just because of his facile ways and language skills, but also by never letting down his guard. Not once in the twenty some-odd years since he left Peru had he ever allowed a single photograph.

Until a dying boy whose pain somehow reminded him of his daughter snapped a picture on his cell phone and sent it to his addled grandmother across the ocean.

\*\*\*

**clairebear** encountered **jtwobears** not in a suicide forum, ironically enough, but completely by chance on a message board thread linked beneath a story on CNN.com about the complex legal systems for allocating water rights in various states.

It was JT who messaged her, thinking she might be of Native origin because of her screen name and the fact that her post was the first intelligent and non-racist comment he'd come across.

He had begun the last stage of his disease, not sleeping at all and drifting in and out of strange delusions. On his good days he went to the club, opened the pool room, then went home to surf the Internet and smoke pot to try and keep up an appetite. On his bad days he never got out of bed, staring at his visions across the ceiling.

His bosses were understanding because Mister Tee was understanding; had he complained they would have had to hire someone to replace JT. But the old man just went back home if JT didn't show by 5:30, and the club manager would open up when he arrived at seven.

Melissa, in her way of drawing out others without revealing much about herself, was soon Facebook friends with the dying boy, who would give her the strength to do that which would both end her life and provide it meaning.

JT told her his story from beginning to end over the course of one long, blessedly lucid night, describing in detail why he planned to kill himself and take Mister Tee with him. A concept inherited from **clairebear**, by way of Charlie.

\*\*\*

JT had become such good friends with the old man that he told his grandmother all about him in long, rambling emails he wasn't at all sure she would understand. Mister Tee, for his part, enjoyed their time together, finding JT the ultimate in safe associations. He was, quite literally, a friend who would self-destruct.

That didn't mean that the old man had lost his edge; to the contrary, he posited whether there might come a moment that would require him to slit the throat or bash in the skull of his new companion, and he knew he would not hesitate if it had to be. It had been a long time for him, but JT was becoming weaker by the day.

Even the thought that he could still take a life if he needed to gave the old man a spring in his step; El Culo was feeling more and more like his old self as JT declined, like Dorian Gray and his painting or a vampire deriving strength from the life of his victims.

Then came the picture.

Mister Tee protested, of course, but not enough, and before he knew it his picture was on its way to the kid's senile old grandmother in a little town in the Basque region of Spain near the French border, known mostly for its slaughter of supposed witches during the Inquisition.

When she viewed the picture on the tiny hospital's computer from her bed at the Consultorio Medico Zugarramurdi, the old woman recognized the face as clearly as she remembered most things from the distant past.

As she looked into the eyes of El Culo de Arica, her blood ran cold, and she ordered the nurse to call the boy in America who claimed to know her daughter.

***

JT explained it to **clairebear** as best as he could, but it boiled down to the fact that his grandmother had known the wife of one of El Culo's survivors quite well, a woman who had lost her only son in a tiny village in the mountains above Lima in a particularly heinous fashion. The man responsible was well known in the city where her friend lived most of her life before she too ended up in Spain. She carried a faded picture of the man who later disappeared, which had been published in the newspaper during Fujimori's bloody war against Shining Path.

She gave the picture to JT's grandmother on her deathbed, extracting no promise to search for him or take revenge, but simply to keep the memory of his crime against her son alive in some way.

JT had not believed her at first, but something in the old man's eyes changed the following day when he asked if he had ever lived in Peru, and then the questions started. JT told Mister Tee that his grandmother said he looked like an old friend she had known from Lima.

It was at that moment that Mister Tee knew he would get to kill at least one more time.

***

JT opened his eyes.

*Have I been...sleeping?*

Mister Tee looked down at him. He was holding a shovel from the tool shed.

"What happened?" JT asked.

"You had a seizure," the old man said cheerily. "Hit your head."

JT looked from his eyes to the shovel.

"Have you been waiting long?"

Mister Tee threw his head back and laughed at that one. He was really going to miss this boy. It had been exhilarating to let someone in again, and in spite of the danger, or maybe because of it, he felt twenty years younger.

The old man helped JT up from the walkway and unlocked the pool room himself. JT noticed, but said nothing about the fact that Mister Tee had apparently rifled his pockets while he was out. He felt a little unsteady, and the old man allowed him to hold onto his arm as they walked inside.

JT collapsed into a poolside chair. He felt like he was going to pass out. He looked up at the old man, who was standing over him with the shovel, smiling.

Jesus Two Bears knew that the tables had turned, and in spite of his bold talk to `clairebear` the night before, he simply wasn't capable of killing the old man. He believed he was an evil man, just as his grandmother had told him, but he just did not have the strength.

"Do you want to say goodbye?" the old man asked, and JT knew exactly what he meant.

"I don't have her number here," JT answered, and even if he did, he had never had very much luck getting her on the phone.

"What time is it there?" the old man teased. JT could see a headless soldier standing behind him, but he knew that wasn't real. His vision was getting blurry.

"Hey!" Mister Tee shouted. "Are you still with us?" He threw down the shovel. There was not going to be any need for it again, which both relieved and disappointed him. He had planned to use the kid's dementia as an excuse, to claim that he had to defend himself, which would have worked but drawn attention to him. This way was better. He could just watch JT die and then call for assistance.

"Just barely," JT whispered. The headless soldier had grown two heads now, which were in the process of eating each other.

"I have her number," the old man said, finally dropping all pretense. He still had people who could get information for him if he needed it. "Why don't I call her for you?"

JT just nodded. He could feel himself slipping into darkness. *I'm sorry, Daddy.*

He jerked his head back from the old man, who was trying to drill into his head with a horned snakehead.

"Talk to her, son," the old man said softly, and JT saw that the old man was holding a phone to his ear.

JT took the phone, but it was the voice of his father he heard.

"Take your stand, boy," he said. "Look it in the eye, and take your stand."

JT dropped the phone, which the old man caught with surprising speed and dexterity. He pocketed the cell and looked down at JT, waiting for a sign he knew what was to come, but JT was silent, his breathing more and more labored.

The two-headed soldier, his faces now half-eaten, rose up into the air and hovered over the center of the pool, emanating a brilliant glow that shone like a spotlight in JT's eyes. He moved his eyes into the shadow of the old man, the light from the soldier now ringed around his head like the halo of a dark angel.

JT tried to speak, but couldn't. The old man nodded, smiling sadly. He had almost wanted the boy to fight, to give him a taste of days past. JT closed his eyes and teetered on the edge of the chair.

"I 'spect the same from you, son."

He opened his eyes. It was the old man's voice now, but his lips were unmoving. The two-headed soldier began to descend into the water, his mouths snapping at each other, newly roused.

JT reached out as if asking for help to stand, and the old man took his hand. JT stood up slowly, then stumbled, and the old man wrapped his arms around him, holding him up.

With his last bit of strength, JT hugged the old man and propelled them both into the pool.

JT could feel the old man's panic as they sank below the surface, and now it was he who derived strength from the weakening of the other. JT opened his mouth and allowed water to rush in, struggling against every human instinct to let go and break for the surface.

He looked into the old man's eyes and saw the evil he was meant to confront. For his ancestors, it had been the 7th Cavalry, for his grandfather, U.S. Marshals, for his father, the bottle.

For Jesus Two Bears, it was El Culo de Arica.

Just before they died together, JT saw Iya the younger float past, his older brother just behind. As the spirits watched him, his entire body relaxed and the struggles of the old man in his arms faded to nothingness. To JT and those who came before him, there was really no such thing as an evil spirit as others might imagine. Without the bad, there can be no good. Without suffering, there is no joy.

All things must balance, and so all things serve their own unique purpose.

The coroner was amazed at the two men found entwined at the bottom of the pool. It would have taken an almost superhuman effort not to struggle against the water and embrace death in the way it appeared the younger man had done. It was almost supernatural.

As the coroner was examining the two men, a very old woman across the Atlantic was feeling particularly happy but didn't know why, and across the country, a very young women felt much the same way, and did.

# 2 MONTHS AFTER TOWY WEBSITE

VALERIE MOSLEY

Two months after 16-year-old Monica Tinsley of Porterville posted her last message on Facebook and then slit both wrists halfway up her arm, police finally arrested three 17-year-old boys on rape and sexual battery charges. It was alleged the former straight A student was brutally assaulted by her fellow classmates while she lay naked, bleeding, and unconscious in the bed of a pick-up truck parked in the garage of one of the hockey players who savaged her. She cited in her final post the cruel texts and cellphone photos of the attack that had been passed around to many other students with whom she attended Turner Woods High School.

But the boys, whose parents all "lawyered up" immediately, were quickly released due to a lack of evidence and, in a sadly ironic twist of fate, the death of a living witness willing to testify against them.

If all this sounds heartbreakingly familiar, perhaps you're thinking of the Seattle case, or the Toronto case, or any number of rapes and sexual assaults whose victims are increasingly wounded again and again by the cretinous use of technology and social media to shame and badger and harass them, this time with tragic and not unexpected results.

But now there appears to be an even greater backlash against such "re-raping", going beyond the posting of the names and private information of the perpetrators to call attention to their oft-unpunished crimes.

A website, towy.la, has begun soliciting people with terminal illnesses and suicidal thoughts to "take one with you" on their way out the door, a kind of purpose-driven death for the Twitter generation, even going so far as to ferret out the names and locations of child molesters and other such vermin. The Turner Three were added just yesterday.

While it seems to me a rather scary concept, as most vigilantism is, I must admit there is a certain horrifyingly beautiful symmetry to the notion that the depressed and dying can feel good about their demise by leaving a better world behind them. 'Taking out the trash' is one of the clever euphemisms the site uses, probably to skirt the legal letter of solicitation laws.

The problem I see is the same problem that afflicts anything when you throw it out into that great big expanse known as the world wide web.

To put it simply, there are an awful lot of crazy people out there. So mark my words: This "take one with you" idea will either fizzle quickly or fast outgrow its debatably reasonable goals.

That's a mighty mean genie to try and coax back into the bottle.

Be slow, my friends.

VM

# Chapter Ten

It was the NSA that discovered Rodney Oscar Thomas was actually Rodrigo Umberto Espinosa, the man responsible for so many deaths and long assumed to have met his own years before.

The FBI initially thought the murder so strange that it warranted a special investigation, particularly because the killer had familial ties to a known domestic terrorist, but it took a FISA court search warrant, a little old woman in Spain with Alzheimer's, and a single newspaper clipping over two decades old to complete the final piece of the puzzle, and it made headlines all over the world.

Later on, when the journals of Melissa Williamson were discovered some time after her death, proof of the connection was made to Jesus Two Bears, who became known publicly as the TOWY Pioneer.

It would also be the NSA that eventually connected them all to Charlie and Sarah, but that information was also kept classified until it was leaked by a disgruntled employee who fancied himself an Edward Snowden but ended up more like a tabloid version of Dan Brown.

The person who made all the connections before anyone, however, was Sarah.

\*\*\*

**u did what?**

Sarah stared at the pm for a moment. She had to smile. Charlie never abbreviated unless he was really mad.

**its good to see u hvnt chngd, chikless**

She immediately regretted hitting send in light of what had happened and what she'd done, but there was no taking it back.

**sorry**

Sarah waited. No response. *Fuck.*

"Come on, Charlie, I said I was sorry."

After the online disappearance of **clairebear**, Sarah had hacked into her login information on one of the message boards, which had led to her email address. From there, Sarah retrieved her private information, address, Facebook, and the like, and that was how she found out that **clairebear** was the same girl who'd been killed in the horrific motorcycle accident with the man who'd killed her sister. It had been a local story, an oddity that had somehow gotten overlooked by national news sites due to a foiled homegrown terrorist bomb plot in Detroit the very same week.

When she looked further, she found the amazing exchange with Jesus Two Bears.

**I can't believe you wrote that.**

*Looks like he calmed down. Perfect grammar.*

**call me we need to talk**

A moment later, Sarah's phone rang.

"I can't believe you hacked her," Charlie said before she could even say hello, but it was obvious he wanted to know what she'd found out, and Sarah was eager to share. She told him everything, from her private conversations with the girl they now knew to be Melissa to what had happened with her sister to what Jesus Two Bears had apparently done.

"What, you mean you haven't hacked him yet?" Charlie asked.

Sarah paused. "I thought I should talk to you, first."

"I'm not your dad," he answered, and like Sarah and her "chikless" text about the death and subsequent hacking of **clairebear**, he immediately regretted his choice of words.

Sarah didn't wait for him to apologize, but immediately jumped in to save him.

"Dude, this is what we talked about."

Charlie went silent. They had indeed discussed such things, mostly in the context of his anger towards both his stepfather and his mother, the former for driving her to suicide, and the latter for not taking him along for the ride. It was amazing to them both that

**clairebear**, who had seemed so shy and reserved online, had actually done such a thing.

She had not wasted her death.

During the time of his estrangement from Sarah, Charlie had had many heart-to-hearts online with **clairebear** and revealed a lot more of his inner thoughts than he had with anyone else since his mother. Even Sarah.

Charlie had considered Sarah a kind of touchstone in his life, one of those people you meet who change you in ways most others don't. Fundamental ways.

He had been very depressed over his relationship with his mother and what he perceived as her inability to see what Brad had done to their lives, but Sarah had snapped him out of that. She had truly affected him. Changed the course of his life.

That was why, even though he initially lashed out at her after his mother's death, Charlie could no more divorce Sarah from his life than he could his mom. They were *intertwined,* he confided in Sarah. Connected to each other.

*"You'll find that, too,"* he'd assured **clairebear**. *"Something or someone that'll wake you up like a cold slap in the face. Someone that changes everything."*

Neither Charlie nor Sarah said anything for a moment. It was obvious they were both thinking along the same lines, although Charlie's thoughts were laced with guilt that he had helped **clairebear** to her death, somehow. He had discussed his dream where his Mom took Brad with her, but also about being woken up.

It looked like this Jesus guy had woken her up, all right. And they were damn sure connected. Briefly in life, forever in death.

Sarah felt guilty as well, thinking back to her suggestion of the tattoo. She'd gotten the idea from her father's last text to her, but she regretted that now. He would not have wanted to be connected to what they'd done in any way.

It was something she'd just have to live with.

Finally, Charlie spoke.

"First off, let's stop calling her Clairebear," he said, and Sarah agreed. They were both in awe of what she'd done and how she'd done it. Far from being a cowardly act, hers had been one they both felt exhibited great courage.

"Unless it's an emergency, or something," Sarah said, more because it popped into her head than from any sort of prescience.

"Agreed," Charlie said. "Melissa from now on." He paused. "It's good to talk to you again, Sarah."

"You too, Charlie."

"So tell me again why you haven't hacked Jesus?"

Sarah smiled and listened as Charlie talked about his idea. She didn't tell him that she had already been all through the email account of Jesus Two Bears, and was waiting for the media to catch up. The connection to El Culo had either been discovered and kept secret, or had not yet been found. Either way, there was no sense in going off half-cocked.

Anyway, she wanted to let Charlie vent a little. He seemed to need it. Plus, he was on a roll with this idea. She even liked the acronym. T.O.W.Y.

Had a nice ring to it.

*** 

Speaking of acronyms, while Charlie and Sarah batted around their idea for a movement to help rid their community of people like El Culo and Big Max, a low level NSA employee in Utah at the newly opened ICCNCIDC, or Intelligence Community Comprehensive National Cybersecurity Initiative Data Center, had found some recent activity connected to a murder-suicide with an interesting domestic terrorism angle.

He walked it down to his supervisor on his bi-hourly fifteen. Fred Dean liked to see his boss' face when he solo'd because he never knew when he was getting an eye roll, otherwise.

"What's up, Freddie?"

"Got something to run by you," he grinned. "On the QT."

His supervisor rolled his eyes. Freddie was always using phrases like that. *Twenty-three and he sounds like some bad 50's detective show.* "Go ahead," he said. Freddy annoyed him, to be honest.

Freddie hated when his supervisor rolled his eyes at him, which he did quite often, which was why Freddie always bothered him in person if he was able, which only further increased the likelihood of an eye-roll, which only further led to the annoyance of them both.

Such was American bureaucracy, even at the NSA.

When Freddie was through explaining what he'd found, his supervisor rolled his eyes and asked him a few questions.

"How'd we get the woman in Spain?"

"FISA, sir."

"And that got this...Asshole character?"

"The Asshole of Arica, yes sir."

"Who's dead."

"Yes sir."

"But you think someone may be...what?"

"Well, I'm not sure," Freddie said excitedly, and sat down in the chair across his supervisor's desk, completely missing the expression on his boss' face as he did so. "But I think I should keep an eye on things in case there's any funny business."

*Jesus. Funny business.* The supervisor rolled his eyes again. "How much time we got on the warrant?"

"Another ninety days, renewable, sir."

The supervisor leaned back in his chair and looked at Freddie. *What a load. No wonder we're getting bum-fucked by Congress, our interns are dumber'n theirs.*

But if he told Freddie to "keep an eye on it," what did that even mean? And if it kept him out of his office for three months, it would be well worth the trouble if he was questioned about it. *No, sir, he had an interesting idea and I just told him to keep an eye on it for the duration of our access. Nothing more.*

"Keep an eye on it, Freddie," he said, and damned if the kid didn't almost leap right out of his chair. *I transfer in two months anyway.*

"You won't be sorry, sir!" Freddie said, and was out the door even before his supervisor could even roll his eyes. *Kid almost saluted me.*

\*\*\*

Charlie and Sarah decided to start with a small website, very unobtrusive, and put out some anonymous feelers in places likely to be frequented, either virtually or personally, by people who were terminally ill. That seemed like a good place to start, with people who were going to die anyway. Before soliciting anyone suicidal.

In spite of his hatred for his stepfather, Charlie's mother had not been sick, only depressed, and Charlie wanted to be very careful with people like her. He knew, in spite of everything, that had his mother been able to kick the prescription drugs, she might have found the strength to divorce his stepfather and change her life for the better, and he would never want to deny someone like that their possible happiness.

That was the reason he had considered suicide himself, because he felt like he failed her. He didn't want to fail anyone else.

But his hatred for Brad was a powerful motivator. Hatred always was.

Sarah wanted to move more quickly, and she made her views known with typical aplomb. "Shit or get off the pot, dude."

"I see why everyone thinks you're such a pain in the ass," Charlie said, and Sarah laughed until she cried. Her father had always called her that, his little pain in the keister, cleaning it up when she was a child and using the unexpurgated version as a term of endearment as she grew older. Charlie could hear her sniffling over the phone.

"You miss him, huh?"

"Don't you?"

They were both quiet again.

"I want to see you," Charlie said.

"I...wasn't sure if you ever would again," she said, leaving unspoken what happened the last time they had met in person, a meeting she had insisted on.

"Are you kidding?" he asked, incredulous. "We're like, connected, dude." Charlie thought Sarah was the most beautiful girl he'd ever seen, and added shyly, "Plus you're totally out of my league."

There was silence on the line and Charlie wasn't sure if he'd made a mistake. In spite of everything they'd shared, he was still very much a typical teenage boy, awkward and unsure about almost every word around a pretty girl.

*Please say something, say anything, just say something.*

"What, you thought you were gonna get some?"

They both laughed, Charlie not quite as heartily as she, and Sarah told him she'd come by the following week. She didn't tell Charlie, but she'd already had idle thoughts of renting an apartment near him. There was a small portion of her inheritance available to her, and she was nineteen now, so why the hell not? Her mother was grieving by spending time with her father's former chief of staff, so they were getting along even worse than before. Charlie was just about the only person she knew who could make her smile anymore.

"It'll be really good to see you, C," she said, and hung up.

Charlie sat looking at his phone. She shortened his name, which was a very familiar thing to do. A tiny little thing, but he thought it could mean something. And she joked about having sex with him, too. *I think.*

"Fuckin' A!" he shouted, and flopped backwards on his bed.

The door opened, and Brad stepped in. "How you doing, Sport?" he asked, in that typically fake, obsequious, used-car salesman type way he had.

"Why?"

"I heard you yelling."

"Are you listening outside my door, now?"

"No, I just thought – "

"I don't care what you think, Brad!" Charlie said, and probably because he always felt somehow bolder after speaking with Sarah, added, "so fuck off."

Brad had been turning to leave, but he slammed the door open again violently.

"What did you say to me?"

Charlie sat up. "Nothing. Just leave," he mumbled.

"What did you say to me?"

"I said nothing!"

"Let's get something straight, pal. This is my house. Not yours. Not your mother's."

"Don't talk about my mother!" Charlie screamed, jumping off the bed as if he was going to physically challenge his stepfather.

"I was married to her!" Brad screamed back. "I can talk about her all I want!"

The two of them stood there, flushed and angry, their chests puffed out and heaving like two boxers before a fight.

"So you got anything to say to me?" Brad asked rhetorically, his obnoxious smirk practically begging to be wiped off his face, something Charlie had dreamed of doing, and worse.

Finally, Charlie backed down, as they both knew he would, and sat on the bed. "Would you just leave, please?" he asked softly.

Brad walked over to the bed and sat down next to him. For a moment, Charlie was horrified. Was he actually going to try and have some sort of father-son moment?

*If he puts his arm around my shoulder, I'm gonna fucking lose it.*

"Look, Charlie. I know you miss your mom, okay? I miss her, too. But she's gone, and we both have to just try and move on."

Charlie said nothing. The only reason he didn't burst into tears was because he was seething. It would not be the first or last time Charlie had been saved by anger, an emotion he was coming to appreciate more and more.

"We just have to move on."

*Stop saying that!*

"Nobody knows why people do what they do," Brad continued, and Charlie really thought he was going to scream.

*Why doesn't he get the fuck out of here?*

"Some people just have problems, you know?"

*No shit, asshole.*

"Sometimes...it's just easier."

"What?" Charlie asked, startling Brad, who had almost been talking to himself by that point.

"Killing yourself," he explained. "Some people just can't take...life, I don't know, and they just find it easier."

"Easier?" Charlie said. "Are you fucking kidding me?"

Brad stood up, and Charlie followed. "I know somebody who better take it a little easier right now."

"Oh, really, Brad? Should I kill myself, maybe?" he screamed. "Like my mother?"

"Calm down, Goddamnit!"

"No, you calm down!" Charlie screamed, and stepped towards Brad, backing him up. "There's nothing easy about suicide!"

"I didn't say it was easy, I said it was eas*ier!*"

"Easier than what, Brad?" Charlie demanded, taking another step and backing him up again. "Easier than letting you take over her life? Easier than watching you fuck around behind her back?"

"I said take it easy!" Brad shouted.

"You fucking killed her!"

Brad, infuriated, shoved Charlie, who fell backwards onto the floor at the foot of his bed. He started to get up, but his stepfather was on top of him in a flash, his red face hot and sputtering.

"You little shit, you don't have any idea what I put up with!"

"What you put up with?" Charlie tried to throw him off, but Brad worked out regularly and outweighed him by fifty pounds.

"That's right, kid," Brad spat. "Your mother was a drug addict!"

"Because of you!"

"She was worthless and weak, and that's why she killed herself, because she couldn't take life!"

"She should have taken you with her!" Charlie screamed. He was crying now, but his anger was such that he had no idea. If he had had a gun or a knife he would have killed Brad right then and there. If his hands were free, he would have beaten him to death with his skateboard or stabbed him with a coat hanger or killed him any way he could.

At that moment, Charlie wanted nothing more than to kill Brad and then himself and end the pain forever.

Brad struggled to hold his wrists. The kid was getting hard to handle. He honestly didn't know what Charlie would do if he let him up at that moment.

"Okay, okay," Brad said, trying to calm things down. "Relax. Just...take a breath."

Charlie looked up at him with the eyes of an animal. The hatred was so intense he couldn't imagine Brad didn't feel its heat. But he stopped struggling. It was hard to breathe with that asshole sitting on his chest, and Charlie just wanted him out of his room so he could calm down and think. He tried to relax his face, to appear as if he was no longer angry, but he didn't want to say anything. The first one of them to speak now would be weak, in Charlie's mind, and the irony of that belief was lost on him.

*Just get out,* Charlie thought, willing his stepfather to leave.

As if he'd heard, or maybe because Charlie's concentration was actually having the desired effect of relaxing his body in spite of himself, Brad let go of Charlie and got to his feet. The boy's wrists were as red as his face.

He stood over his stepson for a moment, wondering whether he should say something. *Jesus, the kid wore me out,* he thought. *I can barely breathe.*

Finally, Brad turned and walked out of the room, purposely leaving the door open as a tiny, childish victory.

*I need to get rid of that little fuck,* he thought as he went downstairs to make himself a drink. *At least his stupid bitch of a mother did one thing right. Thank Christ she gave me some time, otherwise the kid could...fuck.*

Brad shuddered at the thought of Charlie inheriting half his assets.

"'He can't know until he's twenty-one, otherwise he'll get lazy'," Brad spoke aloud in a whiny, high-pitched voice, imitating Charlie's mother. He laughed at the thought of her ignorance, and his laughter swelled, turning into an evil, raspy cough that grew larger, like a snowball rolling downhill, gaining momentum and becoming bigger and bigger until he very nearly choked on the rage that lay just beneath it.

Charlie lay there on the floor for a while, allowing his breathing to slowly return to normal. He heard Brad banging around downstairs for a few minutes and then some massive coughing fit, and then there was silence.

*Maybe he choked to death,* Charlie thought. *Probably just getting drunk in the den.*

Charlie briefly considered waiting until Brad fell asleep and then slitting his throat, but he suddenly wanted to accomplish a few things before he succumbed to that desire.

Sarah was coming over in a few days, after all, and they had plans.

Big plans.

But killing Brad was definitely on his bucket list.

# THE HILL

## Bipartisan House group fails to reach an agreement on TOWY resolution

By Rusty Bachman 11:25 AM ET

Lawmakers negotiating a proposal to curb the growing TOWY movement could not come to terms acceptable to enough committee members to allow the bill into conference. The lower chamber's response to the Senate bill means that TOWY legislation is probably dead for the year. "This was time to be part of the process," a Democratic negotiator, Rep. Candace McMillan (D-Chicago), said Friday afternoon. She added she had been "cautiously optimistic" about the bill's success in the House up until the morning of the vote, when liberal groups such as the ACLU banded together with libertarian leaning conservatives to pressure the members of the committee to vote down the measure. Civil libertarians on the left were concerned the bill would lead to new restrictions on the rights of the accused, while conservatives disliked additional mental health funding included in the bill.

Follow us: @thehill on Twitter | TheHill on Facebook

# **Chapter Eleven**

Sarah never admitted to Charlie that she showed up early on purpose just to fuck with him, and he never came out and asked her, either. But it was pretty obvious that she was used to doing things her own way, and Sarah's way was very often the way that fucked with other people whether it was necessary or not.

It was almost as if it amused her.

He had joked about it with her online, long before they met in person, and she admitted that there was something inside her that liked messing with people, that liked the conflict, *needed it,* and while it kind of scared him at first, there was also something exciting about it. Sexy, even. That was why he had agreed so easily that day to make the drive to see her. Even though he knew his mother was acting strangely.

Charlie hadn't been getting along too well with his mom back then, but he should have known better than to leave her that day. He should have been with her.

Except that he had left. Because he wanted to see Sarah.

Sarah, who was a coiled spring held back with a single pin, always in danger of releasing her kinetic energy your way. Sarah always seemed to be in motion, even when she was standing still. There was an unpredictability that Charlie found incredibly attractive.

She reminded him of an old silent movie he'd watched in school, some Russian film about a mutiny on a ship or something. There was lots of death and dying, and some really cool stuff on the steps of a big building, but what he remembered most was that he never knew what was coming next. There was a tension and uncertainty about it.

Just like with Sarah.

*"I'm more like a hand grenade,"* she'd told him at the restaurant the night they first met in person. *"There's your loose pin, dude."*

They'd laughed and had a great time until the unpredictable intervened. What attracted him to Sarah drove them apart the night of his mother's death.

But it was a separation that proved short-lived.

They were connected, just like Jesus Two Bears and Melissa were. What Charlie wasn't sure of was whether they would remain so. He was acutely aware of what happened to the other "connection".

Charlie stared at himself in the mirror. His mother always told him from the time he was a little boy, that he would grow into his looks. He'd never really understood what she meant until after she was gone. He'd always taken it as a kind of backhanded compliment, like she was calling him ugly, but maybe he'd look good when he got older. Even after she explained what she really meant, he never quite understood until it was too late to share with her.

*"It means I can see the man you're going to become one day, Charlie."* His mother looked at him with sad, wizened eyes. *"I wish sometimes you wouldn't take things so much to heart."*

*He tried to smile, but tears filled his eyes instead.*

*She pulled him close, and unlike so many other times since the death of his father, when Charlie felt too self conscious to fully embrace her, as if being "the man of the house now", as Minister Webber had put it, precluded such gestures, Charlie hugged his mother back so tightly she had to physically loosen his grip in order to breathe.*

*His mother rocked him gently, loving his acquiescence but hating his anguish. After a few moments, she pulled away and held his face in her hands.*

*"You are a kind, sensitive boy, Charlie. And you're going to grow into a kind, sensitive man. The kind of man any mother would be proud of."*

Charlie looked down at his phone. He should have told Sarah to come earlier. Charlie messed with his hair some more, but there was only so much he could do. Then he heard laughter. *Female laughter.*

He checked his phone again. Too early. It couldn't be her. One of Brad's girlfriends. He hated the thought of having to walk past them when Sarah arrived. Maybe he should sneak out the window and wait for her out front.

More laughter. This time it sounded familiar.

*No. Please no.* He cracked the door and listened. He could hear Brad talking, and then...her voice. Charlie threw open his door and ran downstairs.

When he walked into the living room, he couldn't believe his eyes.

Sarah was sitting on the couch next to Brad, and they were sitting really close.

*Really close.*

The three of them just looked at each other for a split second, and then Charlie completely lost it.

"What the fuck are you doing?" he shouted, and for a moment neither of them knew who he was talking to. Charlie wasn't sure, either.

"We're just talking, dude, chill," Sarah said. Her blue jean skirt was very short, and Charlie couldn't help but notice how high it rode up her thighs before she quickly stood up. He hated the fact that she had included the word *just* in that sentence.

Brad remained seated with a stupid grin on his face, as if he was gloating, or something. At least, that was how Charlie saw it. He wanted to smash him with something, anything, to make him stop smiling.

"Ready to go?" Sarah asked brightly, a little too brightly, if you asked Charlie. Sarah was not a chipper person, which made her sound really, really fake. At least, that was how Charlie saw it. He felt like he was in some kind of a carnival funhouse, with everything he heard and saw distorted beyond recognition.

There probably wasn't much of anything either of them could have said or done at that moment that was beyond his paranoid misinterpretations, but he was too mad to allow that fact to derail his focus.

"What the fuck were you doing?" Charlie screamed.

"Charlie, relax." Sarah said.

Hearing that word only incensed Charlie more. Brad had told him to relax the week before in his room just before landing on his chest.

"Don't tell me that!" he screamed.

"We were just talking," Brad said, standing up. Again with the *just*. Whenever someone said they were *just* doing something, chances are they're doing that and a whole lot more. Brad started to move towards Charlie, but Sarah stopped him by *putting her hand on his arm.*

If there was any possible way she could have made things worse besides straddling his stepfather right in front of him, that was probably it.

"That's right, C," Sarah said, stepping in front of Brad, her eyes boring into Charlie's. "We were just talking."

"Stop saying that!"

Sarah suddenly rushed towards Charlie and got right in his face. "That's right," she said. "I was just about to come get you. Now let's go."

There was something in her voice that made Charlie shut up and obey, but he wasn't going to let this go. No way. Sarah took his arm and the two of them awkwardly strode to the front door, side-by-side.

Charlie threw open the door and walked out, but Sarah turned.

"Nice meeting you, Brad," she said, before quickly closing the door, leaving Charlie's stepfather sporting that stupid grin and a guilty erection.

"What do you think you're doing?" Charlie demanded once they were in Sarah's car. She ignored the questions and tore down the street, narrowly missing an elderly jogger who flipped them off.

Charlie closed his eyes and tried to calm down, but it wasn't working. He hated the fact that he was so upset even more than the

fact she had been sitting and talking to Brad. It wasn't even like he
believed there was something going on, it was that Brad had seen
her. Had his eyes on her.

*He's probably jerking off right now.*

Suddenly the car veered to the curb and Sarah slammed on
the brakes, nearly throwing Charlie into the windshield. He'd been
so upset he had forgotten to put on his seatbelt.

"What did you say?" she demanded.

Charlie looked at Sarah, confused. How could *she* be mad at
*him*?

"What?"

"Who's jerking off?"

Charlie's confusion intensified, then turned to surprise. "Did
I say that out loud?"

Sarah stared at him like he was an alien being for a moment,
and then she burst out laughing, and as mad as Charlie had been, he
couldn't help but join her. Every time he tried to stop and bring up
what had happened back at his house, they would look at each other
and start laughing all over again.

It was probably the laughter that made Charlie so
unprepared for what happened next. He should have been ready, he
really should. After all, he'd been thinking of little else ever since
they made the date, which wasn't even really a date, but who cared?
Nobody actually went on dates, anyway, they just hung out.

Hell, he'd been obsessing over it for a lot longer than that.
Probably since they met online.

The point was, Charlie had been imagining the kiss forever,
but he was still totally shocked when Sarah suddenly leaned across
the center console and kissed him.

He kept his eyes open, probably from the shock, but as she
slid her hands from the back of his neck around to his face, gently
caressing him, Charlie felt himself ease into it, like descending into a
warm bath.

Her tongue was full and insistent, alternating between pure
eroticism and playful teasing. She moaned and sucked, and he felt
himself instantly and fully erect. He wanted to move his hands

over her body but instead they fell to his sides like limp noodles, as if to contrast with the teenage monster raging uncomfortably in his jeans.

He felt her body push towards his as she practically climbed into his lap, her arms around him now, pulling him in as if she wanted to force her way through him. Charlie responded with his suddenly working arms, pulling her on top of him. The feel of the bra strap across her back was incredible, his fingers toying with the hook and clasp through the thin material of her blouse.

When they finally allowed space between their lips, the windows of the car were fogged and the only sound either of them heard, in spite of the cars whizzing past on the busy street, was their deep, heavy breathing, synchronized and sensuous.

Neither of them could speak, so they simply held the embrace.

After several lifetimes had passed, Charlie finally found his voice, and the words he spoke made her love him even more than she had only recently realized she did.

"Best first kiss, ever," he whispered.

It was not Sarah's first kiss. As a matter of fact, she was quite experienced in that regard. It was also her experience that most guys her age were braggarts and liars, always looking at sex as if it was some sort of contest, like some video game that gave them extra lives if they scored so many points. They were always trying to impress her, something they had in common with older men, all of them somehow missing the point entirely that she wanted to feel special, and that meant she had no interest at all in prior conquests.

Charlie made her feel special. By simply being honest and open and vulnerable.

Sarah climbed off his lap and settled back in behind the wheel.

"So what do you think?"

Charlie looked at her. He was so crazy in love right then, or maybe just crazy, that at first he thought she wanted him to rate her kiss with some sort of numerical value, like a score at the Olympics.

Fortunately, Charlie thought before he spoke.

This time.

"About what?"

She lowered her chin and looked up through the passenger side window, and he turned around. There was nothing out there, just an apartment building with a sign in front that read *No Vacancy*.

*No Vacancy.*

"Did you – ?"

She smiled and nodded. "I did."

"But…"

He looked around. Sarah had rented an apartment right around the corner. They couldn't have driven more than a few minutes from his neighborhood.

It was that thought that ruined everything. As Sarah laughed and leaned over to hug him, what had happened back at his house flooded back into his consciousness like a sour tide, refilling the void that her amazing kiss had only recently vacated.

Charlie knew he shouldn't say it, but he did, anyway. Like untold numbers of men who came before him, Charlie was about to learn something about women by saying the exact wrong thing at the worst possible time.

The benefit of leaving well enough alone.

He pulled away slightly and blurted out what he was thinking.

"So. What *were* you guys doing?"

Sarah's eyes changed, and he immediately regretted his words. He had taken what was a wonderful moment of bonding and turned it into shit, and there was absolutely nothing he could do about it.

She sat back in her seat and stared out the windshield, grasping the steering wheel tightly.

"Get the fuck out of my car."

"Sarah – "

"Get out!" she screamed, and reached past him for the door handle, yanking it open. He was hyper-conscious of her body even then, her breasts pressed against his thighs for the briefest of moments.

  *Better not say that out loud.*

  "Get out!"

  "Sarah, I'm sorry."

  She laid on the horn, and finally Charlie got out of the car and closed the door behind him. He leaned down and peered in the window, but she refused to look at him directly, turning her face to the opposite window and watching him walk away in the side view mirror through regretful, teary eyes.

# **Chapter Twelve**

Thane downed his third and slammed the glass down on the bar, probably a little too loudly, causing the bartender to glare at him again from the other end of his workstation. The detective shrugged and held up a finger to signal he wanted another while he had the guy's attention, although it wasn't the preferred digit he would normally have used on the little prick. The bartender had been a shit since he sat down, like he was on parole and smelled cop, which he probably did.

*I don't give a shit what you did, dickless. Just fill my fucking glass.*

He watched as the bartender poured him another double Jack.

*Probably queer.*

Thane gave him another look. *Maybe not. Too bad, though. I'd get better service.*

Thane had had words again with his boss, *big fucking surprise*, and had been in a foul mood ever since.

What was really bothering him though, was his ex-wife. She'd been riding his ass about child support even though he'd never missed a payment. The latest burr up her ass was that she wanted him to pay in cash, which he wasn't about to do. Thane had paid her with money orders since the very beginning, closing all their joint accounts and opening new ones in his name at smaller banks she didn't know about.

It probably wouldn't make any difference to her cunt of a divorce attorney if they really wanted to find out his information for whatever reason, but he wasn't about to make it easy for her. As long as she got paid, she couldn't do shit. The two of them could suck his dick.

He smiled as the thought of that image rumbled around in his fevered brain. Thane had to admit that lesbian counselor was a pretty sweet piece of ass, in spite of her fucking disposition. The first time he'd met her in arbitration he'd had wood the entire goddamn meeting. His own attorney kept asking if he needed to get up and stretch or go to the bathroom whenever they took a break, but fuck if he didn't sit there with that raging boner for two solid hours so nobody could read his mind.

He still occasionally rubbed one out to her smug little ass, imagining how it would feel to spread her out for a couple of hours across the mahogany desk in her office he'd probably paid for.

Just then the bartender poured him another and Thane looked up with a dopey grin on his face, causing the guy to roll his eyes and walk away like a felon at the policeman's ball.

*As long as you're around for my rounds, dickhead.*

"Detective Parks?"

*Shit. If I wanted to talk to another cop, I'd fucking pull some overtime.*

He turned around and was pleasantly surprised to see that the voice belonged to Officer Goodbody from the day in the alley with the deaf kid.

*What the hell was her name?*

"Officer Hellstrom," Thane said, standing up and silently congratulating himself on his stellar memory.

She laughed. "Anita, please."

They just stood there looking at each other for the briefest of moments, but it wasn't awkward. At least not to Thane.

It was one of his "quarter moments", as he called them.

The first time he'd ever gone to Las Vegas, Thane was eighteen years-old looking twenty-five, and right away he'd hit triple sevens on a quarter machine with three coins in. That was back when silver actually spilled out when you won.

He'd stood there as his buddies hooted and hollered around him while six hundred quarters poured out, but the thing that struck Thane the most was that he'd just had a feeling the second before that he was going to win. He *knew* that he'd hit before it happened.

Thane had quarter moments sometimes during an interrogation, when he knew all he had to do was shut up and let the perp confess, and ninety percent of the time that's exactly what happened. It was uncanny.

As he stood there looking at Hellstrom, he knew he was going to get laid tonight.

*Nice quarter moment.*

"Call me Anita," she affirmed, and Thane smiled and offered her a seat, which she took. He leaned in close as he sat, smelling her perfume. It was just as intoxicating as the liquor he'd been swilling.

*Good thing I only had three.*

Thane dipped a finger in the freshly poured shot and licked it like a frosting spoon. "What'll you have, Anita?"

"Bottle of water is fine," she said. Thane thought he heard an apologetic note in her voice as if she expected an argument, but he decided against it.

*Never look a gift twat in the puss.*

"Coming right up," he said, smiling. Thane lifted his hand, immediately catching the eye of the wary barkeep once again, who strode over promptly once again.

*Must be my lucky night.*

"Two bottled waters," he said, pushing the full shot towards the bartender. "We're gonna grab a booth."

Thane could tell the bartender was about to say that he'd still have to pay for the shot, but he cut him off at the pass. "This one's for you. On me."

The bartender nodded and then glanced at Anita, who looked pretty fucking hot in a tight red dress and matching heels, with some of that criminal cleavage he'd noticed beneath her eyes.

*Barkeep's definitely not gay. Or maybe Officer Goodbody is just that good.*

The bartender was back in a flash with the non-alcohol, and the two of them made their way to a booth along the far wall.

"So, you hungry?" Thane asked, once they'd settled in.

"Uh, no. Well, I'm meeting a girlfriend for dinner."

*Fuck.*

"Okay," Thane said. "So, where's the old man tonight? Hill Street, right?"

She smiled. "That's right. Didn't know if you'd remember."

Thane laughed. "I always remember the husbands."

Anita giggled and Thane thought he saw a little color appear in her cheeks, too. He was on a roll tonight. Goddamn, he wanted her.

They talked on and on, like it was a first date. Thane noticed after a while that she'd stopped looking around for her friend and seemed a lot less nervous as the night wore on. They ended up ordering dinner, after all. He ordered light.

*Not taking any chances.*

Thane's usual waitress, whose name he could never remember but always laughed when he called her Cookie, gave him a sly wink and nod of approval after appraising Goodbody. For the first time in ages, Thane was just letting loose and having a good time.

Before their food arrived, he noticed that she seemed to be getting a little nervous again, so he flagged down Cookie and ordered them both a drink without asking whether or not she wanted it. Thane had always been a take-charge guy with women, something a lot of them liked, and a few, such as his ex, didn't tolerate for very long.

*She doesn't need to take it very long. Just fifteen minutes or so.*

"What are you grinning about?" Anita asked.

Thane laughed. "Nothing. Just thinking about dinner."

She leaned forward, her neckline now dangerously low. Thane stared into her eyes, which he just realized were an amazing shade of green. If he'd been asked before that moment what color they were, he wouldn't have had a clue even though he'd been sitting a foot away from her for over an hour, but now he was trying extremely hard, not without success, to keep from staring at her tits.

"Tell me something," she said, and Thane leaned in. They were so close he could have shoved his tongue down her throat just

by craning his neck, and man did he want to, but he played it as cool
as he could for a man with a blue-veiner and no place to put it.

Yet.

"What's that?"

"What do you think of Myers?"

Thane blinked. *Myers? Who the fuck is Myers?*

"Chief-of-Detectives Myers," she added, amused that he
looked so clueless about his own boss.

Thane sat back. *Why the fuck did she bring up Myers?*

"Right," he said. "Myers." He nodded, appraising her anew.
*What the fuck is her angle, anyway?*

"I'm just wondering because of that night," she added
quickly.

"What night?"

"The boy. In the alley. The deaf – "

"Right, yeah, I remember," Thane said. "The kid in the alley.
Myers was there." He leaned in again. "Why, what did Myers do?"

"Well, he was kind of an asshole," she answered, and that
was all she needed to say. Thane opened up like that long-ago
quarter slot machine, filling her in on all the past slights he'd
suffered at the hands of the higher-ups like Myers who'd been
holding him back for so many years.

Anita Hellstrom just sat back and listened for the better part
of an hour as Thane raged against the department in general and
Myers in particular. Their food came and went, barely touched, as
Thane told her his secrets and lies, his hopes and dreams, his fears
and ambitions.

And she began to feel empathy for him, which surprised her.
Thane actually seemed like a good man and a loving father, although
pretty rough around the edges. Her own dad had been like that,
gruff and quick to anger, but when the chips were down, he knew
who his friends were and he would fight for them with all he had.

Thane seemed like that to her. A man with his own particular
code of honor that didn't necessarily match up ethically or even
morally with that of society's, but which was a code nonetheless, and
there was something to admire in that. Her husband was shallow

and ambitious, more like Myers, in her eyes. A man who would easily rise above his level of competence over time simply by being a good politician. A man who knew which asses to kiss and how long to hold his pucker.

Thane was not a politician, she could see that now.

"Shit, what time is it?" she asked.

"Hell, I don't know," he answered, looking around for a clock, then comically searching his pockets for his cell phone.

"Thane."

He looked up. *Goddamn she's got some beautiful tits.* "Yeah?"

She reached across the table for his hand, and he was about to lean over and just fucking kiss her, when she grabbed his wrist and turned it over to check his watch.

Anita looked up at him with a confused look, and he chuckled.

"I don't wear watches that work."

She just stared at him for a moment. "Okay, you're gonna have to explain that."

"Nah, it's okay," he said, and turned to look through the pockets of his coat for his cell.

"Tell me," she said playfully, "you told me everything else."

Thane looked up a little too quickly, and she could see another side of her father, the side she didn't like as much. She could see a flash of something more than anger, something closer to rage. At that moment she refocused and batted her eyes and smiled, and the madness drained from his eyes as quickly as it had appeared. When he started to speak, she could breathe again.

"I had this watch once. A gift from my ex, back when we were still married. I kept wearing it after the divorce, I don't know why."

He looked at her almost sheepishly, and seeing in her eyes what he believed was real compassion, continued.

"So one day it stopped working. I don't know when, but it made me late for a very important meeting, and...things got all fucked up. So now, I don't rely on any goddamn watch to tell me what time it is."

He smiled and shrugged. "Stupid, huh?"

"What was the meeting?"

"It doesn't matter."

"So why do you still wear the watch?"

"This? This isn't the same watch," he said. "Hell, no. Different watch."

"So why do you wear *any* watch?" she asked. "If you don't use them to tell time?"

"Fuck if I know," he said. "Just feels like a man should wear a watch, I guess."

She laughed. Now he sounded exactly like her father.

"What's so fucking funny?" he asked, laughing with her.

She shook her head. "I'll tell you when I know you better."

He liked the sound of that. Thane reached in his coat, finally finding his phone, and said, "Eleven-forty."

Her eyes widened, and she reached into her purse, frantically digging through it as if she didn't trust his cell phone like he didn't trust his watch.

"I have to go."

"Oh, okay. Sure," he said, the disappointment evident in his voice. "I'll walk you out." He threw some bills on the table. *So much for my fuckin' quarter moment.*

"That's okay, you don't have to rush out because of me."

"Like I'm gonna stay in this dump," he said, and they walked towards the door.

A dark figure in a non-descript sedan a half block up the street sat up and took notice as they exited, taking a last drag of his cigarette before tossing it, where it landed amongst several other butts on the damp pavement.

There was a light mist coming down, so Thane quickly took off his jacket and held it over their heads as they walked towards her car. She quickly fished out her keys and unlocked her doors with the fob.

When she turned, he was on her, kissing her passionately, and for a brief moment she responded.

Thane's hands were on her neck, surprising her with a gentleness that belied his hungry lips, and moved up to caress her face.

She managed to get her hands between them and pushed him off as politely as she could. "I shouldn't," she said.

Thane pulled back, but only slightly. He looked deeply into her eyes, staring until it made her uncomfortable. "You're lying," he said.

She just looked at him, frozen.

"You want to," he said. She said nothing. "You know you do."

"I have to go," she said. "Really."

"Aw, fuck it," he said, and turned away. But he didn't leave. When he turned around he was holding the watch in his hand.

"It's the same watch," he said. "Same goddamn watch. The meeting was to take my kid to the movies. For his birthday."

She reached out and touched his arm, but he didn't seem to notice.

"Bitch waited five minutes and left." He looked up at her, and she saw the rage in his eyes again. It was like she wasn't even there. He might as well have been talking to a complete stranger. "Five fucking minutes late, and I missed his birthday."

Suddenly he turned and threw the watch, where it clattered in the street and came to a rest very near the pile of cigarette butts near the sedan. She followed it with her eyes and then looked at the dark man inside, whose eyes she couldn't see but which she knew were boring into her.

She grabbed Thane and spun him around, pulling his face to hers and kissing him with a desperation that shocked him in its ferocity.

He started to reach for her body, but she pushed him away, and without another word, got into her car, slammed the door, and drove away.

Thane just stood there for a moment, watching as she turned a corner and disappeared out of sight. He felt his wrist and looked up the street toward where his watch must have landed. He briefly considered retrieving it, but then decided against it.

"Fuck it."

Thane walked back to the parking lot, got in his car, and left.

After he was gone, the dark figure in the sedan started his engine and slowly rounded the corner, lights off.

*VARIETY*

SIGN IN  Google™ Custom Search  🔍   *Subscribe Today!*

FILM +    TV +    DIGITAL +    VOICES +    VIDEO +    SCENE +    VSCORE +    MORE +

HOME | BIZ | NEWS

# Errol Morris to Helm TOWY Doc For The Weinstein Company After Personal Pitch from Harvey

EMAIL    22    44    207
PRINT    TALK    👍 +1    🐦 Tweet    📘 Share

Gary Neil

MOST POPULAR

*1*

# **Chapter Thirteen**

Charlie walked home after his argument with Sarah stunned and confused. He had just experienced his first kiss and his first real fight, all in the space of about thirty seconds, and he didn't know what to think.

It was times like that he really missed his mom.

Losing his father young had made him, for lack of a better term, a mama's boy, something he'd been called at school as an insult, but which he fully embraced in practical terms. All it meant to him was that he was especially close to his mother, and he never saw anything wrong with that.

Charlie always felt like his dad's passing was a gift, in a way. A dark gift he would have preferred never to receive, but a gift, nonetheless. In death, his father left him a legacy of maturity he might otherwise have taken years to attain.

It made sense, of course. Being thrust into the role of "man of the house", *whatever that meant*, at an early age had a tendency to either set a boy on one of two paths: responsibility or recklessness. While he had always considered himself on the former, it sometimes seemed like a fool's errand. Charlie had a hard time making friends, and had never, before Sarah, had anything close to a girlfriend in his life. He knew it was partly his fault, but he also believed that his failure to relate to others was because he'd grown up just a little faster than his peers.

By the time he realized that everyone had a persona they showed the world, and many families had unhappiness and tragedy they chose not to reveal, he had pretty much set his course as a loner.

He went to a high school party once and stood in the corner all night, pretending to be a tortured soul when all he really wanted was one of the girls he'd watched from across the room to approach and engage him in conversation. To be curious about him, curious enough to come over.

None did.

Soon enough he came to understand you had to be careful about what you pretended to be, because that was often what you would become, like it or not.

It was his mother who always moderated the extremes in his personality. If his father's death had allowed him to grow up fast, it was his mother's life that had allowed him to just be a kid.

Her loss was more devastating than his father's.

And now he had lost Sarah.

Of course, he hadn't really lost her; they'd only just had an argument. And he wasn't at all sure he'd ever *had* her, in spite of the kiss. All those years by himself in his room had rendered him clueless about the behavior of others, sometimes.

Being so inexperienced with girls, Charlie wasn't at all sure about what he was supposed to do. All he knew was that hearing her scream at him like that was the worst feeling in the world, and he never wanted to feel that way again.

He called and texted her several times during the short walk back to his house, but she never responded. He considered walking right back over to her apartment building, but decided against it.

*Maybe she just needs a day or so to cool off.*

Except he couldn't do it. He knew he shouldn't text her, but he did it anyway, several times a day. It felt so desperate and pitiful, but he just couldn't help himself. Charlie was incapable of artifice. He wore his heart on his sleeve, and so could not leave things be.

Still, she never responded.

Nights were the worst for him. There was something about the wee hours that intensified his emotions. That made things seem entirely more hopeless and overwhelming than they would be in the light of day. And even though he understood that intellectually, Charlie simply could not own it emotionally.

He was, in a word, miserable.

Or as some would say, in love.

One night about a month later, things got particularly bad for Charlie. Terrible thoughts raced through his mind, feelings of guilt and loss related to both his parents, and shame that he had allowed Sarah to render them both somehow lesser in importance in the pantheon of his guilty conscience.

He hated the fact that he thought of her more than his folks, now, but he had to admit that he did.

After his father died, Charlie often dreamed he was still alive. In his dream, Charlie was always older than his years. He would be spending time with his father, and the penultimate moment was always a handshake, and they were always the same height, which seemed of paramount importance. After the handshake, his father would turn and walk away, and then Charlie would wake up. This dream was strangely comforting.

Charlie was relating to his father man-to-man, which would never have actually happened outside his dreams.

Then when his mother died, Charlie began to dream of the night she killed herself, except in his dream, he arrived home in time to save her.

Since his fight with Sarah, all he dreamed about was Sarah. She was always standing over him in a flowing gown, much taller and older than himself, as if he was a child and she a mature woman. She never spoke, only looked at him with an exquisitely intense sadness, and then she would float away and disappear as he strained to reach out and touch her. Sometimes he would feel the delicate hem of her gown slip through his grasp, and other times the garment was like smoke through his fingers, impossible to hold.

The result, however, was always the same. Sarah was gone, and he was alone.

He began to resent her in his waking hours, as if she'd been a force that had somehow destroyed the peace he didn't actually possess. He had avoided Brad and Brad had done likewise ever since his outburst, and as a result Charlie was more alone than he'd ever been, without even Brad to remind him to hate.

In an odd way, he missed that hatred, and wanted it back almost as much as he wanted Sarah. He felt like he had committed the ultimate betrayal of his mother. Not only had she been pushed aside by his feelings for Sarah, but Charlie was now living almost harmoniously under the same roof with the person most responsible for her death.

Something had to change.

Then one night he woke up from his dream with the perfect solution to his misery. It had been there all the time, of course, but somehow it had always seemed slightly abstract, like an equation he had to memorize and would remember all his life but never use. There was no planning required, no preparation as he'd always believed. All he needed was the will, which had arrived suddenly and without warning.

Charlie practically leaped out of bed.

Was this how it was for others? He had no idea. But he knew that he had to, as the saying goes, strike while the iron's hot.

Charlie laughed. *Another perfect idea.*

He grabbed his phone for illumination and walked out into the hall, past Brad's bedroom, and went downstairs to the living room. He saw what he needed. It felt good in his hands. It felt *right*.

Charlie felt incredibly light on his feet. He made no effort at all to remain quiet, but very nearly skipped up the stairs by the eerie light of his cell phone. It was an incredible relief to have finally made the decision. He had no idea what he would do afterwards, well, he knew *what* he would do, he just didn't know *how* he would do it.

But now he knew that he could, and that made all the difference.

Charlie opened Brad's door, the moonlight from the open window glinting off the brass poker he'd taken from the fireplace downstairs. The heft of the implement gave Charlie comfort. Brad always liked to buy the most expensive of everything whether he actually used it or not, and this was a fine example of his hubris.

He stood in the doorway for a moment, savoring the peace that had come to him so suddenly. Charlie almost couldn't wait to bury the sharp hook in Brad's skull, if only because he imagined Sarah's reaction when she heard the news of his murder-suicide.

They had talked about such things so often, and now Charlie would have her undying respect.

*Undying. Maybe that's the wrong word.*

He laughed, and Brad stirred in his sleep, but Charlie wasn't worried. It would almost be better if he woke up. That was the one tiny flaw in his plan. That Brad wouldn't see it coming. Charlie really wanted Brad to see it coming.

As he stood in the doorway contemplating whether or not to wake up Brad before staving in his fucking skull, Charlie was almost tingling with anticipation. His entire body was practically vibrating.

Charlie looked down. It was a text.

He lowered the poker, which he hadn't been aware he'd raised, and brought the phone to eye level.

**fu chikless**

Charlie stared at the screen, not noticing that Brad had just opened his eyes, not quite comprehending what he was seeing: A silhouette in his doorway, holding some sort of weapon.

Charlie turned and left the room.

***

"What the fuck are you doing?" He threw her report on his desk in disgust.

Anita Hellstrom just stared at the Chief of Detectives sullenly, not quite knowing what she should say. Undercover work was all pretty new to her, and she wanted to tread carefully if she could.

"I'm not sure what you mean, sir."

Myers laughed derisively. "Tell me how this isn't just a goddamned waste of resources."

"I just got started, sir."

"Shit," he said, almost spitting out the words. "You came to me on this, officer."

"No I didn't!" Anita said. He really caught her off guard.

Myers narrowed his eyes. "I mean you came to me about the deaf kid," he said. "Which, by the way, amounted to dick. The kid never repeated any of that shit about Parks going after the homeless guy."

"I can talk to him again. He trusts me."

"Too late for that. The homeless guy disappeared."

"So why did you put me on Parks, then?" she demanded. "Sir."

"Watch your tone," Myers growled. He stood up and walked to the window, as if considering just how much to tell her. From the beginning, Anita could sense some of the higher-ups had it in for Thane, and based on what the deaf boy had told her, she was all for taking him down.

After spending time with him, however, her thoughts on that were a bit more conflicted. She trusted the kid's version of events, but maybe Thane had a good reason.

He'd jokingly mentioned "taking out the trash" once or twice, as in cops who were known to be exceptionally rough and even murderously violent with certain perps, much like the prison hierarchy that demanded retribution for certain offenses. Maybe Thane knew something about the homeless guy they didn't.

Myers turned around to face her. "Look, I need you to get closer to him."

"Captain – "

"You practically blew him when you left that bar a couple weeks back, for Christ's sake!"

Anita flinched as if she'd been slapped, and stood up. "Fuck you." She turned and headed for the door, but Myers caught her hand on the knob. She whirled around, backing him up. "And why were you tailing me that night, anyway? I follow him and you follow me? Is that how it's done? Jesus!"

"Anita," he said, almost but not quite apologetically, "sit down."

She turned and shot daggers his way, but followed the instruction. Myers let her stew for a minute before continuing.

"What's the problem?" he finally said.

"I'm married!"

"I cleared it," he said, visibly exasperated.

"You *cleared it?* With who?"

"Who do you think?" Myers asked, and looked like he immediately regretted it.

She looked at him, incredulous. "You brought my husband into this?"

"I gave him a heads up so there wouldn't be any problems," Myers said. "I'm looking out for you."

She laughed bitterly. "Thanks for your concern."

"I'm looking out for both of you! John wants to make detective, you want off the streets. How the fuck do you think you get promoted around here?" he scoffed. "Merit?"

"I guess Thane learned that pretty quickly, huh?"

Myers glared at her. "Maybe you're right. Maybe you've spent too much time with him already." He stood up as if to dismiss her, but she quickly reconsidered. She wanted to advance, and she knew this was the quickest way.

"Fine," she said. "I'll stay on him. It's just awkward, you know?"

"Yeah, he's got a thing for you, I got it. Part of the job."

"Why can't I just shadow him?" she asked.

"We tried that. He picks it up. Got a sixth sense for that shit." Myers sat down. "That's why Internal Affairs closed the books on him. But he's got something going on. I got instincts, too."

"Whatever works, though. Right, Captain?"

"Of course. I'm just trying to keep you from wasting your time, that's all."

"I understand," she said, and stood up to leave.

"Anita," Myers said, stopping her at the door. "You get something solid, I can run with it. I don't give a shit how you do it. Just be careful. Parks is good."

"How good?" she asked.

Myers grimaced, as if he might choke on the words. "If he ever learned how to play ball, you'd be spying on the next Chief of Detectives."

She nodded and walked out, closing the door behind her.

***

Thane looked at the return text from Anita.

**`Cant 2 nite. Raincheck?`**

"Goddamnit," he yelled, and almost threw his phone out the window. This chick was driving him nuts. She'd been putting him off for weeks now, and he knew damn well she wanted him. All that accidental lust, and then nothing.

*Accidental.*

Thane had wondered at first about how she just happened to show up at the bar like that, but their conversation that night had pushed all that to the back of his mind. There was something raw and honest about her, and though he wasn't used to that in a woman, he found it extremely affecting. Anita had brought out that same raw honesty in him, and it surprised him how much he wanted more.

She gave him hope.

Still, he wasn't about to let some piece of ass completely cloud his judgment. He'd gotten through an official investigation recently after he'd "borrowed" some buy money from the evidence room after a drug bust he had no idea would go to trial so quickly, barely replacing it, misfiled, so that it looked like someone else's mistake. But he'd had to go to a loan shark to get it back that fast, and it hurt. The fucking ex had been putting the screws to him for spousal support and money for the kid, creating emergencies that would look good in court, trying to get him to fuck up so she could deny visitation. She was the reason he took the money in the first place, the stupid cunt.

The whole thing with the Internal Affairs' shooflies left him even more suspicious of other cops than he already was.

Anita, however, was different.

*Why the hell is she putting me off?*

"Aw, fuck it," he said, and left the house for a scum run. He liked to keep tabs on the ones that got away, just in case the opportunity for a little off-the-books justice presented itself. That's why he let loose on that asshole in the alley. Stealing from a kid like that pissed him off, but because he'd been under investigation, it had been a long while since he'd risked going out. The candyman had just been in the wrong place at the right time.

Thane pulled up outside the titty bar and cut the engine. One of his lucky rapists was known to frequent the place, so maybe he'd get lucky too and catch him for a beat down. Thane hadn't killed any of them yet, mostly just scared them the hell out of the area, but he was feeling the old rage building up, and since Officer Goodbody wasn't letting him aboard, maybe he'd find another way to blow off a little steam.

***

Anita Hellstrom pulled to a stop a half block away and waited for Thane to get out of his car, but instead he just sat there outside the strip club, like he was on a stakeout. She had found herself oddly disappointed when she followed him there, as if they were in a relationship or something. When he didn't get out of his car, she was not only curious, but also absurdly relieved.

"Come on, Anita. Focus."

She watched him for another hour before anything happened, and it was nothing like she expected.

After the bar closed, the patrons filed out, followed shortly after by what were obviously the dancers, some alone and some in small groups. The last girl to leave was escorted to her car by a bouncer, who then got in his car and drove away.

Anita watched as Thane stared at the girl, sitting in her car and lighting a cigarette.

*Oh, Jesus, no,* Anita thought.

But then a seedy-looking character came out of nowhere and yanked open the dancer's car door, and that was when Thane flew into the parking lot with his torch, catching the guy in his spotlight just as he was about to hit the girl.

She watched in fascination as Thane cuffed the guy and threw him in the back seat of his car, then leaned in and said something to the girl before letting her drive away.

*He's not calling it in. If this was official he'd need her statement.*

Anita followed him as Thane drove around, seemingly in circles, which told her that he was being exceedingly cautious, so she hung back as far as she possibly could and still keep eyes on the vehicle.

After another forty minutes, Thane led her to an industrial area and disappeared between the warehouses. There was no way she could go in there without being detected, so she parked down the street and waited.

A half-hour later, Thane's vehicle exited the complex the same way he'd come in. There was only one person in the car.

Anita waited until Thane's car disappeared and then drove into the parking lot and slowly made her way around the decrepit-looking buildings.

She found him almost immediately.

The guy from the strip club was lying next to a trash bin in a fetal position, as if he'd been trying to shield himself from an attacker.

*Oh shit.*

Anita pulled her service revolver, suddenly aware that she might not be alone with the guy. It wasn't the best neighborhood to get caught with a corpse. Or anything else, for that matter.

Then the guy moaned, and she ran towards him. She kneeled down and rolled him over. His face was swollen and bleeding, but he was conscious. She found his wallet and wrote down the guy's name. She noticed he had more than a few twenties in there to go with a cache of ones.

*Lousy tipper.*

Anita ran to her car and sped away, stopping at a convenience store with a pay phone, and called it in anonymously. Then she drove past the warehouse until she saw the ambulance and a cruiser, and went home, exhausted and intrigued.

When she ran the guy's name the next day, she was convinced that, despite the beating he took the night before, he was one of the luckiest scumbags she'd ever seen.

His arrest record was longer than her arm, but there were no convictions. She decided not to tell Captain Myers, though. At least not yet.

*This might be bigger than some missing buy money.*

# **Chapter Fourteen**

**`Child molesters`**.

Charlie waited, staring at his phone.

Nothing.

He texted her again, this time with three more words he knew would get her interest even more than the jarring phrase that came before, a bastardization of one of the ancient rap songs they'd laughed about online before they'd met in person.

**`Hack tha police`**

His phone rang and he nearly dropped it trying to answer.

"Leave me the fuck alone, asshole!"

"Unless you don't think you can do it," Charlie challenged. He felt like he was treading a very thin line, but he'd not forgotten how to push her buttons.

"Fuck you," Sarah said, but she didn't hang up, and Charlie knew he had her.

"Instead of finding them online, why not go straight to the cops' files? Throw a few locals to get things started."

Charlie waited in silence as Sarah considered that. The plan was, before their fight, to put up the TOWY site and start with a list of people they'd gotten from the state sex offender registry, then keep watch in newspapers and social media for cases that fit the criteria: people who deserved to be punished, but were beyond the reach of the legal system. But with access to local police files, they could surprise some people who might otherwise go unnoticed. Scumbags who thought they were safe.

"We can watch," Sarah said.

"Exactly," Charlie replied. It was eerie how they were so in sync, sometimes.

"We find the lucky ones," she said, sounding more and more excited. "The ones who *think* they're getting away with it."

"The ones nobody knows about," Charlie added. "Except the cops."

There was another long silence on the other end of the line, and it was all Charlie could do to keep from screaming into the phone, but he managed to stay quiet. It was almost like she was testing him, taunting him, waiting to see how long she could keep her response, and herself, just out of his reach.

That only made Charlie want it more, something they both knew.

On second thought, Charlie decided she knew how to push his buttons *a lot* better than he did hers. Probably all girls did.

"Hey," she said, her voice soft and urgent.

"Yeah?" Charlie answered, trying and failing to sound nonchalant. *She so owns me,* he thought.

"What the fuck are you doing over there?" she demanded more than asked, and then she was gone.

Charlie hung up and jumped in the shower. He was so excited he could barely contain himself, but he still wanted to be nice and clean in case...well, just in case.

It was not, however, only the possibility of Sarah's body against his own that so inspired him. Even more importantly, his plan for the website and how it would all come together was falling into place even more perfectly than he'd hoped.

He did feel a little guilty for keeping a certain part of his plan secret from Sarah, but he was pretty sure she would approve if she knew. And she would know, eventually.

But as much as he loved her, and he *did* love her, he knew that now, that was one particular detail he couldn't share with anyone, not even Sarah.

At least not yet.

That didn't mean they couldn't have a little fun in the meantime. *Hell, maybe she'll let me move in with her. Better bring an overnight bag.*

\*\*\*

Brad took another drink and stared out the window. *Does he know?*

He ran his hands through his hair, rubbing his scalp like a Magic 8-Ball, but there were no answers forthcoming.

"The fuck am I gonna do?"

He'd been a nervous wreck ever since he'd woken up with his stepson standing over him with a poker. Not because he thought the kid actually had the balls to do something, but because he *didn't*. At least, he hadn't when he had the chance. But he was still worried.

In Brad's experience, if you wanted to hurt somebody but didn't have the guts, you'd eventually find some other way to do some damage, and there was something strange about how Charlie had been acting lately. Something was up with him, and Brad thought he knew what it was.

The day after Charlie's friend Sarah came by, Brad had gone down to his office to retrieve the document. A document that basically returned control of his entire business back to him. A document his wife, Charlie's mother, had signed not long before she died, not knowing it would rob her precious son of his inheritance.

The arrangement had worked beautifully for a while, but more and more Brad had realized it had all been a colossal mistake. It would have been easily fixable, though, except the stupid bitch jumped the gun. Things would have looked a little too suspicious if he'd recorded the document so soon after her suicide. Like he was purposely trying to fuck the kid out of his inheritance.

Which he was.

Brad didn't need anyone looking too closely at his wife's death, however. Especially all those prescriptions he'd filled for her at multiple pharmacies, using multiple doctors.

"Goddamnit!" Brad screamed, suddenly so agitated he could barely contain himself. Everything would have been so perfect if the dumb bitch could have just held on a little longer until he had everything in place.

Brad paced around the room, wishing the kid was in front of him so he could strangle the little bastard.

After several minutes pacing around the house like a caged animal, Brad finally began to calm down enough to focus on the problem at hand.

*Why should the kid get half just because I went temporarily insane for a piece of ass that passed its sell-by date before our first anniversary?*

It had all gone so smoothly till that night. The cold shoulder, the extra pills. He'd planned on a few more months of slowly nudging his wife towards the edge, all the while moving undeclared cash from his insurance scams back to his accounts at a rate the feds wouldn't notice.

But she'd proven to be even weaker and more worthless than he realized.

It had been such a perfect plan, using his wife's name on whatever documents he needed to provide himself deniability if he was caught, knowing she'd be dead by the time that happened, if it ever did. She couldn't be forced to testify against him while she was alive, and he would be protected after she was dead.

Brad had been almost giddy when he'd gone down to the office after a respectable period of mourning to retrieve the paperwork to file with the court that essentially tied up the final loose end, his erstwhile stepson.

But when he opened the safe in his office, the document was gone.

Brad couldn't believe it. He must have put it someplace else. He had to have that document. There were only two people on earth that knew of its existence, and one of them was no longer *on* the earth, but *in* it.

*Fucking bitch. She got it, somehow. How the fuck did she know? There were dozens, maybe hundreds all told, and she signed every last one in a goddamned drug-induced stupor.*

*How the fuck did she know to take that one?*

What all this meant was that Charlie owned half of Brad's assets, including the business he'd started twenty years before, and Brad couldn't do anything about it. He couldn't even transfer those assets now without attracting attention to what he'd been doing.

Brad stared out the window.

*Did he know? Did Charlie have the fucking thing?*

The kid had been antsy lately. One minute he looked like he owned the world, and the next like he was about to follow in mommy's footsteps.

*If only.*

"Goddamnit," Brad seethed. "Kid's gonna take my business."

*Unless...*

Brad rushed back to his study and pulled out the center drawer of his desk. He looked at the .38 for a moment, then moved it aside and picked up the old business card beneath it.

Brad grabbed his phone and dialed the number on the card, which had been given to him over ten years ago by a former business associate even shadier than himself who warned him not to use it unless he absolutely had to.

*"Last resort, Brad," his partner had told him. "He doesn't like to be bothered unless you're serious."*

*I'm serious, all right,* Brad thought. *Serious as a heart attack.*

"Hello?" a gravelly voice said.

"I have a problem," Brad said, and picked up the revolver, placing it in his pocket.

As Brad hung up the phone, he heard Charlie bounding down the stairs, and impulsively staggered out of the room and lunged for the front door, beating Charlie by a foot or two.

Charlie stepped back warily, his smile turning to a scowl.

"Where do you think you're going?" Brad snarled. His hand was fingering the .38 in the pocket of his robe.

Charlie noticed and shook his head in disgust, assuming Brad was fondling a bottle of something. *Asshole is still wearing his fucking pajamas at two in the afternoon.*

"None of your business."

"You fucking piece of shit," Brad said drunkenly. "I'll make it my business."

"Get out of my way," Charlie said.

"You gotta do what I say, asshole. This is my house."

"Not for long," Charlie said, and was surprised when the color seemed to drain from his stepfather's face. He was very nearly shaking, and for a second Charlie thought the man was going to pass out.

Until he looked deeper into Brad's eyes.

He wasn't shaking because he was unsteady; Brad was shaking from pure, unadulterated rage. Charlie had never seen such visceral hatred in another person's eyes, although had he ever looked into a mirror on one of those nights he lay awake thinking of what had been done to his mother, he would have seen it in his own.

Brad moved his hand in his pocket, and for a crazy moment, Charlie thought he was going to offer him a drink. There was something in his eyes that made Charlie think whatever Brad was fumbling with was for him.

Then something hit Brad from behind in the leg, and he very nearly jumped out of his skin, whirling around to face the door as if he thought he was being attacked. Charlie took his chance and rushed past him, opening and slamming the door behind him before Brad could protest, running past the postman and up the street.

*Safe to assume the jerk won't let me use a car.*

Brad looked at the envelopes on the floor, and then stumbled to the window, watching him, not realizing Charlie's last words had been in response to his first demand, and not the second.

*"You gotta do what I say, asshole. This is my house."*

*"Not for long."*

At that moment, Brad knew that Charlie knew his secret, or at least he thought he knew, which was effectively the very same thing.

***

The two of them were up all night putting the website together, and it was the next morning before either of them realized they had barely spoken the whole time, merely taking turns at her laptop, making corrections and tweaks until everything was perfect.

"towy dot la," Sarah said, turning the screen directly toward Charlie as the morning sun streamed through the window behind them. "Awesome."

Charlie stared at the page, then clicked through the other pages, with mocked up names and pictures of future assholes, which would be followed by pages devoted to user profiles and forums for those users to discuss others to be added to the list.

The forums were the most important part, actually, in Charlie's opinion. He wanted the pedophiles and murderers and rapists he imagined populating the site to get what was coming to them, but even more, he wanted the idea to spread. Not because he thought it would make the world a better place as Sarah believed, although he kind of agreed, but because he needed it to be big. Big enough to contain his secret, the one detail he was keeping from Sarah, both for her own good and because he didn't want to scare her off.

In an odd way, Sarah was a bit of a purist with her mayhem. Charlie figured she was willing to be the catalyst for the murders of people she had never met, but if she knew what really motivated him above all else, she might not go along.

Charlie just didn't quite trust her with his life just yet.

They made love for the first time once the website went active, and for the second, third, and fourth time after that over the course of the afternoon. Charlie counted every time and told her he would continue to do so for the rest of his life, remembering each and every touch and smell and taste and curve of her body.

"Every last kiss," he promised, his eyes as wide and sincere as a curious child, which, in a sense, he was. "I'll never be with anyone else."

Sarah smiled when she heard those words, but she didn't let him see. She knew full well there would be others for them both, but there was beauty in the illusion and she had seen far too much ugliness in her life.

"Neither will I," she lied, unaware that there was another lie between them, a lie she would never have suspected given the way they had spent the last several hours.

As wizened as she saw herself and as innocent as she saw Charlie by comparison, there was something inside him that was like biting on tin foil, something cold and unreachable that he was right to hide from her, something that even the heat of a first love could never thaw. Something that would have genuinely frightened her.

Charlie had been forever changed by his mother's death. He had always been a sweet-tempered kid, a product of two parents whose personalities joined together perfectly to produce a soul as gentle as their own, but something had begun to turn after his father's death, and he had only recently discovered just how deeply he'd been affected by the added loss of his mother, which seemed to have completed his dark transformation.

What he was keeping from Sarah was something he had been denying to himself ever since they first began to discuss life and death and Melissa and Jesus Two Bears, something that seemed too awful to contemplate. But recent events had forced him to admit what was driving him all along. The final lie he told himself, the one which he still clung to, was that he would be able to tell her eventually, and that she would understand.

They spent most of the next three days alternately hacking into police computer files and adding to their memories, but it would be the last time for a long while they would have the luxury of such time to themselves.

Once the website gained attention, things would begin to move very quickly, beyond even what they both expected and what Charlie had hoped for, and events would soon spiral out of their control.

# The Greenv

# 3 Bodies Found After Fire

Arson investigators discovered three bodies in the charred remnants of a house in the Windham Heights section of Greenville yesterday. A demolition crew was in the process of clearing the debris in the days following the three-alarm fire that destroyed most of the structure when a construction supervisor noticed what appeared to be human remains. The bodies were missed during the initial investigation in spite of reports that neighbors testified hearing gunshots just prior to the conflagration.

Investigators were called back to the scene and recovered the unknown persons. "Identification is pending, and may be difficult due to chemicals involved that caused the fire to burn extremely hot," GFD spokesman James Fleischer said. "All we know at this point is that there were three of them." Public records indicate the property is owned by Bradley J. Connor, but Fleischer refused to confirm whether police had any other information regarding the owner or his whereabouts.

Ren
foll
imp

The
tha
rela
the
bel
of a
exp
in li
its
bel
cor
or v

It n
tot
thi
dec

# Chapter Fifteen

"It seems to be connected to this goddamn website. The victim's picture was posted just a few days ago, so there's that, and the weird symbol the perp drew on his own stomach before he offed himself matches a picture on the site. We don't know what the hell it means, yet."

The watch commander turned back to the screen and scrolled down to where the crudely drawn picture had been uploaded by Charlie and Sarah only days before. It roughly matched the tattoo Missy had gotten in a West Covina, California strip mall some time before she attempted to take out Big Max, who was, ironically, now residing in a convalescent hospital only a few miles from the tattoo parlor Missy had visited the day before she scrambled his brains and severed his spinal cord.

"He drew it in the victim's blood, by the way," the watch commander continued, still scrolling through the site. "Upside down. Guy wasn't bright enough to, you know, do it right-side up for us. Or, whatever."

There was scattered laughter until a cop in the back brought up what they had all been thinking.

"So do we award this douchebag a medal at his grave, or what?"

The laughter swelled and turned to applause as the watch commander turned around to face the room with a tight grin on his face.

"Look, we all know the vic was a sex offender – "

"Fucking pedo!"

"No shit, Sherlock," the watch commander said, taking back the room with his tone. "It's on the Internet. We all know what he did. But he also did his time, and he registered every year, and this is still a murder investigation, all right?"

"What's to investigate? Perp's dead."

"Captain's worried about copycats. This fucking website's already getting a lot of traffic, and there's a lot of chatter from these morons about who's gonna be next."

"I got twenty on the Captain," a cop in the back whispered loudly, which caused both laughter and a few nervous boos.

"All right, knock it off!" the watch commander yelled, and this time the room got quiet and stayed that way. "You know that viral shit. Something like this could get out of hand if every dickhead with nothing to lose decides to off somebody. We don't know if this guy was actually meeting with other like-minds, we don't know shit. There could be a fucking clubhouse for all we know. So far it's local, so keep your eyes and ears open. You see this symbol anywhere, or hear anything about 'taking one with you', call it in. All right?"

"Hey, Sarge." An officer in the back raised his hand as if he was in school.

"Yeah?

"Is that website even doing anything illegal?"

The watch commander sighed. "Probably not. Maybe some hacking."

"And it's on the Internet, like you said, so..."

"There a point coming anytime soon, Chang?"

"Well, if whoever put up the site was looking for this result, and it goes viral, there's not much we can do about it, right?"

"Jesus, Chang, why don't we just fucking close up shop and let the lions in? I said keep an ear to the ground. It's one thing to go out and kill a child molester; it's something else to fucking organize it in my backyard."

\*\*\*

It was only a day later when the second murder-suicide occurred, and to make matters worse, the bodies were discovered in an alley just two blocks from the police station. The victim was another local name taken from the state's registry of sex offenders, whose information had been posted on the TOWY website.

At this point, most of the rank-and-file were silently cheering that another local pedophile had been delivered from their midst, but the governor's office took notice as the details of the crime were leaked and the heinous cause of death drew national attention.

The man had been choked to death with his own testicles.

\*\*\*

"What's so goddamn interesting about the task force?" Thane asked angrily, startling Anita with his sudden aggression.

The two of them had just finished a perfectly adequate meal around some perfectly adequate conversation, and Thane was feeling mightily pissed off.

"Excuse me?" Anita said, returning his attitude. She'd been moving slowly, trying to keep his libido at bay while keeping him on the line, which had been looking more and more frayed as the days passed. She used her husband as an excuse when she could, but Thane could easily check the assignment schedules at any precinct and figure out when he was working, so it was getting more and more difficult to put him off.

On top of that, she was beginning to want him as much as he wanted her, which was even tougher to deal with.

Anita hadn't taken kindly to Myers' little meeting of the minds with her husband, which made her feel like some kind of whore. Basically her boss had gotten the okay from her husband to pimp her out if that's what it took to prove Thane was dirty, a situation that had put a terrible strain on their marriage.

*"What the fuck did you tell him, John?"*

*"Nothing!"*

*"Bullshit!"*

*"Just that it was okay. You know, you could, like, work him."*

*"Work him?"*

*"Like a case. A suspect."*

*"I don't fuck suspects, John!"*

*"Who said anything about fucking? Jesus!"*

*"That's what Myers thinks!"*

*"I never said that, Anita. I didn't."*

*That's the problem. Nobody's saying it, but everybody's thinking it.*

"Anita. Baby." *He put his hand on her shoulder, but she angrily shrugged it off, and her anger was infectious.* "Look, you want to move up, don't you? Get off the street? Well, now's your chance!"

*John stormed out, probably to fuck around out in the garage with his miniature car collection, a hobby she secretly loathed, and Anita waited until she knew he was gone before she started to cry.*

"You mean *your* chance."

"What?" Thane asked. "What do you mean, *my* chance? Chance for what?"

Anita looked up at Thane, whose face now held more confusion than anger. *Shit, I said that out loud.*

"I just meant it could be your chance for a promotion, you know, heading up the task force. Especially if this thing blows up."

Thane looked at her for a moment and then sat back in his chair. He'd been so wound up he hadn't realized his fists were planted on either side of his untouched dessert and he was leaning in like he was about to jump across the table.

"They'll never promote me," he said, and slumped back in his chair. The truth was that his interest in the task force was mostly because he was fascinated by the premise of taking out the trash, as the website called it, and it meshed with his "extracurricular activities" of late. The things he did in secret that he told no one about, things he was sure he'd take to his grave, in spite of the fact he knew others in his position must have felt the same way at times.

What Thane had always hated most about the job were the ones who got away, the ones he knew were guilty but he couldn't prove it or got off on a technicality. And suddenly there was someone out there with a plan that perfectly encapsulated that terrible feeling and turned it on its head. Someone who was doing what Thane had always fantasized about. He'd even kept a list of his own with the names of those he thought deserved punishment for crimes that were officially unsolved, although his recent forays into the night were more an anomaly than a habit.

In spite of everything, Thane still believed in the system. The system that had chewed him up and spit him out, the system that had been his life, the system he could never leave, never divorce, never abandon. In his heart he told himself that the system was everything, that justice was paramount, and that things would always work out, but lately he'd been wondering if it was all just a lie he told himself to get through the days and nights that were starting to bleed together.

And then he met Anita, who seemed to bring out something in him that he'd always held in check. His emotions. Thane's ex had always called him the Statue, as if he was made of stone, and there was more truth to that nickname than he liked to admit. What began as a little joke between a husband and wife had eventually become a chasm neither could cross. He hated her for leaving him, but he knew that their break had been mostly on him.

It was ironic that by the time he met a woman who could revive his passion and bring out his best, he was getting too old and cynical to allow himself to break free of his self-constructed prison.

And of course, she was married. That had never bothered Thane before, but that was because he'd never really cared before.

Anita watched as Thane almost seemed to deflate before her eyes. She could almost feel his conflicted feelings on the subject of the task force. Maybe it was because she'd seen the results of such inner turmoil after he nearly beat to death that rapist who'd gotten away with his crimes for too long. Regardless, she sensed that the reasons he'd volunteered for the task force, *campaigned* for it, were deep and confusing, even to him.

There were also more sinister theories, theories that Anita dared not think about too long, but nonetheless danced around the dark recesses of her mind like busy moths around a campfire. She told herself that Thane was not capable of such things, but that may have been a lie she told herself to excuse her own attraction.

Like those moths, Anita felt herself drawn to the flame.

Thane was everything her husband wasn't, tough and open and emotional and *there*. She could feel the passion come off him like a blast furnace whenever she was with him, and more and more had come to realize that she wanted to be in the middle of all that heat.

Anita knew it was wrong, and she was probably as conflicted about Thane as he was certain about her, but one thing she knew for sure: Thane would never have had a conversation with her about 'working' a suspect, or anyone else, for that matter. Not even to get ahead in her career, especially considering his own. He'd basically fucked himself because he was too stubborn to kiss ass, and that was something she respected. As she had often marveled, Thane was a man like her father, a man she sensed was a straight shooter in spite of his many faults, a feeling that grew stronger within her every time he was around.

She realized she was staring at him, and was suddenly aware of his eyes burning into hers.

Anita was almost breathless at that moment, and then they both stood up, together, each of them wordlessly acknowledging what they both knew was to come. Thane threw some cash on the table and they made for the door, bursting into the cool night air with an anticipation neither had experienced for quite some time.

That night they made love with urgency and abandon, with an almost feral intensity that carried them through to the morning and beyond. Neither of them thought of any of the complications that would follow, or the task force, or the system, or any of the obstacles most certainly headed their way. They only felt the call of their flesh, their sweat, their bodies, their needs.

For a few hours, those needs were more than met, and neither of them knew or perhaps even cared at that moment that it would be the last time they were, together.

# Chapter Sixteen

It was the thirteenth officially verified TOWY murder-suicide in Greenville that cause the movement to go viral, led to the conflagration at Charlie's house, and enabled the low-level NSA analyst to put all of the pieces together that would eventually allow the world to learn the full story behind one of the strangest socio-criminal enterprises the world had ever known.

Ironically, Charlie and Sarah, the creators of said movement, were probably among the last in the city to hear about it.

It was perhaps because the national news media and blogosphere had been obsessed with another partisan battle in Congress and a hostage standoff involving American oil workers in Nigeria that the developing series of deaths took so long to garner national attention, but when it finally did, it did with a vengeance.

Charlie had not been back to the house he shared with Brad since the day he and Sarah first made love, and it was their lovemaking that prevented them both from realizing, for a short time, exactly where they went wrong with the TOWY movement.

***

"When are you ever going back?" Sarah asked, not because she wanted him to, but because she knew he had to, and the sooner he did, the sooner they could get started on the rest of their lives together.

"I don't know," Charlie answered, outlining her nipple with his finger, a gesture that made the hair on the back of her neck stand up. He leaned over and kissed her, his lips opening only slightly to allow her tongue to push them apart in that awesome way she did when he was moving too slowly, which, so far, was every time they had sex.

This time she pulled away, which was unusual only because she had never done so with him in the weeks they had been together.

"You have to get more of your shit, dude," she said, and he removed his hand from her breast and rolled over onto his back, staring at the ceiling.

"Right."

Sarah turned on her side and moved her leg across his body, pushing in close and rubbing herself against his warm flesh. She took his hand and guided it back to her breast, the two of them kneading the soft flesh with fingers intertwined.

"I didn't mean right this minute, chickless."

Charlie laughed and rolled on top of her, moving himself between her legs and kissing her full on. Besides a virgin, the one thing he was definitely no longer, was chickless.

***

Thane was on the scene more quickly than the other murders because this time the Towy had sent a text to some goddamned news reporter, but he probably would have been dispatched whether or not it was immediately known to be a TOWY case.

It wasn't every day that a bomb went off in a residential neighborhood, known more for its speed humps than its crime statistics.

The scene seemed like something out of Iraq, and it was probably a miracle that the TOWY farmer, in addition to himself and the pedophile whose name he'd plucked from the website, had taken out only a single innocent bystander.

A four year-old girl had been walking with her mother, who released her daughter's hand mere seconds before the blast so she could run ahead and look at a squirrel that was sitting in the middle of the shady sidewalk, its bushy tail high and twitching as if it knew something much more dangerous than the girl was fast approaching.

The squirrel turned and ran up the gentle slope of a well-manicured yard just as the little girl's eye caught something else, a man sitting in the driver side of a blue SUV, who appeared to be crying.

Their eyes locked in the instant before they both died, and each initially reacted to the sight of the other according to their nature. The man saw what might have been, a potential victim to his sick obsessions. The girl saw only tears.

The mother, once she was released from the hospital in the wheelchair she would need the rest of her life, told anyone and everyone that her daughter had had an almost sixth sense about the suffering of others, and would sometimes drag her over to adults they did not know, perfect strangers, offering them a hug and a smile and telling them that things would be okay.

*"Feel better,"* her daughter would say, as if she knew of some inner heartache. It was the first sentence she'd ever put together as a toddler.

The scene rocked Thane to his core. Thanks to the text, the media had arrived before the cops, almost simultaneous to the blast, and it was chaotic just clearing the people out of the area to survey the scene. There were dozens of people standing in the street, most of them with cell phones, eager to take pictures of the carnage and pass it amongst their social network like some viral venereal disease.

"Get those fucking people back!" Thane screamed at two uniforms, one of whom had what looked like vomit down the front of his otherwise impressively turned out shirt. They were trying to put up police tape while people were running back and forth to the smoking hull of the twisted vehicle. Firefighters and paramedics were on the scene, as well, treating several onlookers. "And that goddamn tape should be all the way back at the corner!"

At that moment, Thane wished he could bring back the asshole with the homemade bomb just so he could kill the guy himself. He looked up and saw four separate helicopters, all jockeying for the best vantage point from which to obtain that perfect blood-soaked, long focus shot through the trees that lined the street on either side and formed a semi-canopy over the wide, suburban street.

He also wouldn't have minded taking out the creator of that fucking website. He'd been vaguely intrigued by the idea at first, like many others, but this was taking things too far.

Thane walked over to the first officers on scene, both of whom saw him approaching and waited with grim expressions. He could see several body parts only a few feet behind them. He had a fleeting thought that perhaps everyone should move away, that there could be a second blast, which was a typical tactic of terrorist bombings in other parts of the world to draw in a second wave of victims, but he discounted it immediately.

There would be a second wave of victims, all right, and then some, but this was not the work of terrorists. This was something else entirely, something a little scarier.

This was regular people who'd just had enough.

***

As Thane was talking to first responders not far from where the coroner was collecting two sets of intertwined arms and legs, Charlie and Sarah were making love for the second time that day. Their cell phones were on mute and the laptop on which they'd created the beginnings of such havoc was turned off for the first time in weeks.

They each wanted to explore the other's body uninterrupted by the events of the outside world.

***

"It looks like they were embracing each other at the moment of detonation," the coroner said drily, speaking to Thane as his assistants carefully loaded the human remains into special zip lock bags like so much road kill. He noticed Thane's expression. "Budget cuts," he said, and the detective immediately understood why they were using veterinary bags for the body parts, although he would have advised against it.

As he might have predicted, there would be a minor scandal after that particular bit of information came out during the Grand Jury proceedings months later, but Thane held his tongue. He was more interested in what the coroner had said before.

"What do you mean, 'embracing'?"

***

Charlie and Sarah were locked in a lover's embrace, their bodies smooth and glistening and molded together. Had one been hovering above the bed, it would have been hard to tell where one body began and the other ended.

***

"They were holding each other," the coroner explained. "Hugging."

***

She slid Charlie back inside her easily, as easily as he'd slipped out. She was straddling him now, moving to her own rhythm and pace, grinding herself against his pelvic bone to try and orgasm. He relaxed and let her move atop him, content to let her take control and merely grip her thighs and thrust upward when it felt right. It was amazing to Charlie how she could almost lose him and then pull him in again, just when he thought he was out.

***

Thane just looked at the coroner and again held his tongue. The perp was obviously hanging on for dear life because the pedo was trying to get out of the car before the explosion.

***

Sarah put her arms around Charlie's neck and hugged him tightly, grinding her hips against his in a tight, circular motion. He could feel her clench around him, which made him harder. He hoped she was going to come because he didn't think he could hold out much longer.

"Wait for me," she whispered, her voice husky and hot against his neck.

***

"I'd rather not wait any longer," the coroner said, and Thane shrugged his shoulders and released him with a look. The asshole was going to catch hell for those doggy bags and probably lose his job, anyway, why should Thane make his last months on the job any more uncomfortable than they had to be?

He called one of his officers over and told him to send the DNA kits directly over to the coroner's office and ride along with the doomed son of a bitch and wait with him until forensics got there. Truthfully, he'd rather do all that shit out of the public eye, anyway. *Sick fucks are mesmerized by this shit.*

*** 

They climaxed together, or almost, anyway. The important thing was that they both came, arriving at the same place in close enough proximity that it felt like they'd passed some necessary milestone in their relationship. A sexual marker.

Sarah, the more experienced of the two, was more excited than Charlie, though the event was acknowledged by them both as a special moment in the way that young lovers mark such things. She knew just enough to understand that it didn't happen all that often, whereas Charlie seemed to take it in stride and even look at it as a harbinger of things to come.

He had always been the more outwardly hopeful of the two, although inside, his darkest thoughts far surpassed her own.

After they almost came together, Charlie figured they simply weren't totally in sync yet, but there would be many years to get things right.

That assumption, above all, was probably what sealed their fate, since it was his hope for their future that changed his mind about things, and which caused him to share those dark secrets he had, until that afternoon, kept so carefully hidden.

And so it would be trust that would bring them down, and love that would destroy them.

Excerpted From Unsealed Indictment, Los Angeles County, California

## SUPERIOR COURT OF THE STATE OF CALIFORNIA FOR THE COUNTY OF LOS ANGELES

### S57814

The People of the State of California,

CASE NO. BA235772

Plaintiff
v.
John Michael Davis

## INDICTMENT
### COUNT 1

The said JOHN MICHAEL DAVIS is accused by the Grand Jury of the State of California, County of Los Angeles, by this Indictment, of the crime of MURDER, in violation of Penal Code Section 187(a), a Felony, committed prior to the finding of the Indictment, and as follows:

In the County of Los Angeles, said JOHN MICHAEL DAVIS did unlawfully, and with malice aforethought murder Lawrence Gonzales, a human being.

"NOTICE: The above offense is a serious felony within the meaning of Penal Code Section 1192.7(c)."

"NOTICE: Conviction of this offense will require you to provide specimens and samples pursuant to Penal Code Section 296. Willful refusal to provide specimens and samples is a crime."

The Indictment continued along those lines with the names of two more victims, all reputed members of the Alwood Street Locos. The primary evidence of guilt was a cell phone video uploaded to YouTube showing the father of a twelve year-old boy whose birthday gift, an iPhone, was allegedly stolen by the victims, who allegedly had bullied the boy after school on several previous occasions.

The day before he allegedly gunned down the three men, John Michael Davis, a working class man with a history of violence and emotional instability, visited a tattoo artist in West Covina who had become well known in certain circles for recreating an image he had originally designed for a repeat customer about a year before, a pretty but sullen young woman who first inked her body in honor of her older sister, Claire.

# Chapter Seventeen

The man in the windbreaker just looked across the table at Brad, who didn't think he looked much like a hitman. Not that Brad would have known, outside of the movies, what a hitman was supposed to look like.

"How do you know the kid knows?"

"Excuse me?"

The man in the windbreaker sighed heavily. He didn't like this guy the moment he spoke with him on the phone. Even before that, actually. His caller ID had given his real name, for starters. What kind of idiot called someone like him from his goddamn home phone?

"Look, Mister Smith," the man said, using the name the idiot had given *after* calling from his unblocked home phone, "this is not something you undertake lightly. As a matter of fact, it's something to be avoided if at all possible."

Brad sniffed. "Are you trying to talk yourself out of a job or something?"

That was another thing he didn't like about Brad. Everything he said came out like he was talking to an employee, which technically, he was not, at least not until he'd accepted the job.

Which he was, at the moment, disinclined to do.

He leaned across the table and gave Brad *the look,* and waited until he either spoke or returned his gaze with something that showed at least a modicum of sober caution and propriety he expected from all clients who hired him to kill people.

Brad opened his mouth and then shut it, as if he was finally thinking before he spoke.

*Okay, I'm staying. But just.*

"I actually don't know for sure," Brad answered finally.

"Then may I suggest you do a little investigation and make certain, because what I do is permanent and involves a bit of risk."

Brad's eyes narrowed. "For whom?"

*Whom. Jesus Christ, everything about this guy bothers me.*

"Who do you think, Mister Smith?"

Brad blinked. "Both of us?"

The man in the windbreaker smiled. "That's right. And I like to mitigate my risks, which means I'm a last resort kind of guy. I'm the guy you come to when there's no other choice, because that is a motivating factor for most people. I appreciate properly motivated clients. Clients with no other options. You seem like a man with options."

"I can't afford to wait," Brad whispered. "He could ruin me if he knows."

"And yet you don't even know where he is."

"I thought...maybe you..."

The man in the windbreaker just stared at Brad as he stammered out the words.

"Doesn't that come with the service?" He asked hopefully. "I could add in some kind of...finder's fee."

The man shook his head. "When you find out where he is, call me back," the man said, standing up. "It's not imperative that you know everything he knows, but a motivated client probably would have that information, and I appreciate – "

" – properly motivated clients," Brad finished, causing the man to briefly smile, a feeble thing that barely survived the atmosphere of his craggy, serious face and never quite reached his eyes. For the first time, Brad noticed how scary-looking the man was, and decided that windbreaker or no, he definitely looked like a hitman.

Brad stood up, too, and there was an awkward pause as he tried to decide whether to shake hands with his potential murderer-for-hire.

The man in the windbreaker grabbed his hand and pumped his arm once, like a casual acquaintance of recent inception.

"Keep in touch," he said, smiling, and turned to leave the restaurant.

Brad just stood there, as the man assumed he would. *Guy doesn't know whether to shit or wind his watch.* The man in the windbreaker was almost to his car at the far edge of the parking lot before Brad realized he was standing in the middle of a bustling diner and staring into space like a complete fool.

As soon as he sat down, a pretty waitress with dark hair and brooding eyes came up to the table. "What else can I get you?" she asked, slightly sullen, and it was at that moment that Brad knew not only how to find Charlie, but what to do when he found him.

Maybe he wouldn't need the man in the windbreaker, after all.

\*\*\*

"When the fuck were you going to tell me this?" Sarah said, her voice rising.

"Why are you so upset?"

"Because you lied to me!"

Charlie couldn't believe how badly the conversation was going. Here he had finally figured out women, and now this.

"I didn't lie," he said. "Not really."

Sarah threw off the sheets and jumped out of bed, and the pungent smell of sex and sweat wafted out into the open and nearly overwhelmed him. He wanted two things so badly he could barely contain himself from screaming out at the top of his lungs. A shower, and to go back in time two minutes and take back his "confession", or so she was calling it.

Sarah just stood there, naked, watching him squirm. It was like she was daring him to allow his eyes to crawl over her body so she could hit him with that, as well.

"Not really," she repeated, sarcasm practically dripping from her lips. *"Not really."*

"Hey, I said I was sorry!" he shouted, starting to lose it. Five minutes ago he would have answered, if asked, that he thought he could have taken anything she said or did without any complaint whatsoever, so strong was his love for her. Now he felt himself slipping into some sort of angry abyss she seemed determined to pull him towards for no reason other than that she could, and there was nothing he could do about it.

He knew what was happening, but he was powerless to stop himself.

And *now*, he understood that women, and other matters of the heart, were not to be 'figured out' at all.

"You dragged me into this – "

"What are you talking about?"

" – because you didn't have the balls to kill your stepfather!"

Her words stung him because they made him seem petty and weak, and because it was mostly true. He wanted to build the website because he basically planned to slip Brad's name on it without her knowledge, in order to entice someone else to do what he didn't have the courage to do himself.

He just looked down at the floor, feeling the disgust in her eyes, and it was at that moment that, for very different reasons, they both realized the import of what they had actually done.

It was one thing to speak of the website in an academic sense, to rage and quake against the pedophiles and rapists and murderers who went unpunished for their crimes. To pretend to be callous and tough as their generation had learned to be in an online world without real world consequences, but several real people had died for their sins.

But whose sins?

In spite of their crimes, those hated human beings had been warm flesh and hot blood and solid bone, who would never again draw breath because of their website.

And what about the innocent people that were perhaps coaxed into murder and suicide?

Everything that had come before suddenly welled up inside the two of them and threatened to spill out like the blood of the farmed.

What they had been doing together the last several weeks while they found more and more names to judge, names from the state website and names from stolen police files and names from the local newspapers; it all seemed obscene.

They'd been tasting each other and feeling each other and sucking and fucking and playing and laughing while others took the lives and deaths of other human beings into their hands like so much clay, molding them on the whims of children, which was suddenly how both of them felt. Like imperfect, immature beings with no certainty of emotional advancement.

Neither of them spoke, but they each became acutely aware of their nakedness and began to get dressed in silence, like two long-ago partners after eating from the Tree of Knowledge.

After they were clothed, Charlie fired up the laptop and Sarah turned on the TV, and the founders of the TOWY movement, by way of a dying Native and a disconsolate sister, saw just exactly what their arrogance and naiveté had wrought.

# Chapter Eighteen

**How are you holding up?**

It was the first time in days Anita had actually been able to get hold of Thane, even by text, what with the FBI coordinating efforts with the local TOWY task force. The death of the child by car bomb had suddenly turned a microscope on everything, and Thane had been working twenty hour days to try and find whoever was responsible for putting up the website.

**Same old shit**, Thane typed in response. He was in the middle of another naptime briefing, trying his best to ignore the FEDSAC, otherwise known as the Federal Special Agent in Charge, or as Thane called him, the Nutsack.

The Nutsack hated it when he texted during meetings, so Thane tried to do it as much as he possibly could.

Plus, he hadn't gotten laid in weeks and he was feeling it.

**Anything I can do?** ☺

Thane smiled.

**Wtever you want, baby.**

God, he wanted to get her back in the sack.

But surprisingly, he didn't just want to fuck her. He wanted to *be with her*. He missed talking to her, even over the phone, which had been rare of late. He missed her smell, her touch, her taste. Thane had not even washed the shirt he'd been wearing the last time they were together, taking it out of the closet and sniffing it when he got home sometimes like some goddamn Brokeback cowboy.

Anita had laughed like hell over the phone when he'd told her that. A year before, he'd never have considered sharing something so silly, mostly because it would have never crossed his mind in the first place.

The truth was, she'd changed him.

Even more surprising, he didn't mind. Son of a bitch if he didn't love her.

Thane looked up and saw that he'd pushed the Nutsack about as far as he dared in a single day, so he signed off with Anita and focused on the briefing, which was pretty much nothing but horseshit.

The problem with the FBI, as far as Thane was concerned, was everything. In this case, they kept him on as joint head of the task force, local edition, but it was clear that he was just around in case they needed a scapegoat. His only real power now was using his own investigative skills and a few back channels even the Feds didn't pay attention to, to try and get a break in the case.

It was an unusual task force in that there was basically no perpetrator, but about a billion *possible* future actors, and the FBI didn't generally do so well with crime prevention when there wasn't a person to actually chase. The whole thing was more for show, as far as Thane was concerned, but that didn't make it unimportant. On the contrary, the Feds were scared and it showed through in everything they were doing.

Some of their bean counters had obviously run the numbers and came up with a computer model that told them if they didn't get a handle on things pretty quickly, this would turn into the first real world, viral murder spree.

Because of the notoriety of this, the Feds had a sealed John Doe warrant for whoever had put up the website, who were thought to be locals based on the content and thought to be young, based on their skills.

The TOWY site had been hosted until recently on The Pirate Bay, a notorious and secretive site that was banned all over the world but also had proxies all over the world, and whose founder, coincidentally, had recently fallen under suspicion for his own murder-for-hire activities.

The Feds knew that was bullshit, but they weren't about to clear the poor bastard just in case they needed a scapegoat on the other side, which was another reason Thane didn't trust them. The guy was going down for something, the Feds just hadn't decided for what.

The warrant for the TOWY site founder or founders would never hold up in federal court, but for the time being the Attorney General had come up with a tortured legal reasoning to allow it, and when the person or persons were caught, something else could always be cooked up.

It was rumored that the Pirate Bay creator had also started the TOWY website, and there were other unsubstantiated rumors, as well. Some said there were Biblical prophecies that foretold the phenomenon, a kind of play on the old eye-for-an-eye, with a "newly discovered" ancient scroll that changed the translation to "an eye *with* an eye", or some such crap, and others that it was the first sign of the apocalypse, that those who killed would come back to life like the fictional inhabitants of a popular television show.

There was even a version related to chemtrails and fluoridation, passed around on Twitter and Facebook much like the actual entreaties to rise up and take someone out if the opportunity arose.

All of the crazy theories developed over time, morphing anew and combining and recombining with each other until all semblance of sane discussion on the topic of the Towys seemed to be relegated to the impotent jurisdictional bodies and governments who seemed powerless to stop it.

Over time, the TOWY movement became a mirror reflecting whatever ugliness or saintliness or retribution or mercy that resided within the TOWY farmer, and there was all of that and more. The world economy hadn't helped either, with feelings of hopelessness and despair contributing to the cause. New studies had found a correlation between hard times and suicide, findings that were disputed by many, and the TOWY movement was just another log on that particular fire.

No academics of consequence thought TOWY was actually driving up the numbers, but no one had ever seen anything like TOWY before.

People were choosing to take their life and the life of another for reasons as varied as there were people willing and able to join the movement.

All of this weighed heavily on Sarah and Charlie.

In truth, they agreed to take down the site as soon as they saw the news reports of the death of the child, but it was too late. Sarah had initially set up the site through a torrent site in Laos, sending encrypted files using Tor, but in just hours after the death of the toddler it had been mirrored hundreds of times around the world, through The Pirate Bay and others, eventually numbering in the thousands. Soon enough, the name and design had been appropriated by others, most of them quickly shut down, but just as quickly replaced.

All of this made the federal task force even more worthless since the originators had no more control over their "followers" than over the tides of the ocean or the clouds in the sky, but something had to be done, and by God, the government was going to do it. Whether or not it actually solved the problem.

Besides, there was always the faint possibility that the founders had a hand in their imitators.

In the course of several weeks, Charlie and Sarah had gone from confused and angry teenagers to loving soul mates to the focus of a worldwide manhunt. Unless somebody stepped in, they both knew it was only a matter of time before they were caught.

Their last afternoon of sweetness together, the same day a child was blown to bits by someone they'd inspired, turned out, much like two other lovers in their city, to be their last.

What brought them together had torn them apart as quickly and as easily as they had fallen into bed, and events had made it impossible to ever call back the genie.

Charlie and Sarah, like Thane and Anita, would live and die with the consequences.

# 1 YEAR, 8 MONTHS AFTER TOWY WEBSITE

**From eyewitness accounts and Congressional Transcripts, House Judiciary Sub-Committee on Crime, Terrorism, Homeland Security, and Investigations, the Honorable Elizabeth Ross-Levy presiding:**

Ms. Ross-Levy: *I would like to welcome everyone back from lunch. Please take your seats. Thank you. Mr. Bronwyn, you reserved the balance of your time, are you ready to proceed?*

Mr. Bronwyn: *Yes, Madam Chairman.*

Ms. Ross-Levy: *Thank you. Dr. Matthews, are you ready for a few more questions?*

Dr. Matthews: *Yes.*

Ms. Ross-Levy: *Thank you, Doctor. Mr. Bronwyn, you may proceed.*

Mr. Bronwyn: *Thank you, Madam Chairman. Dr. Matthews, during your previous testimony, you stated that you'd changed your mind regarding the treatment protocols recommended by the World Health Organization, is that correct?*

Dr. Matthews: *That's correct.*

Mr. Bronwyn: *And you're aware the CDC has adopted the same set of recommendations, as well as the Justice Department?*

Dr. Matthews: *Yes.*

Mr. Bronwyn: *May I ask why? You were instrumental in the early adoption of these protocols, for the prevention and treatment of these people, the ones that failed, were you not?*

Dr. Matthews: *If I might explain –*

Mr. Bronwyn: *Please, because frankly, I'm baffled.*

Dr. Matthews: *Of course. When I first met with one of the, as you called them, failures, I was intrigued because he didn't appear at first to fit the criteria we'd seen in the early cases. All previous cases, actually.*

Mr. Bronwyn: *How so?*

Dr. Matthews: *As you know, the initial cases were primarily random, perpetrated by depressed individuals who were, for lack of a better word, 'inspired' to bring meaning to their lives –*

Mr. Bronwyn: *You mean deaths, don't you doctor?*

Dr. Matthews: *I suppose you could put it that way.*

Mr. Bronwyn: *Depressed people who were going to kill themselves anyway. Sometimes due to a terminal illness or what have you, these Towys started killing pedophiles and such before they committed suicide.*

Dr. Matthews: *Uh...well, yes.*

Mr. Bronwyn: *Until this one fellah.*

Dr. Matthews: *Yes. With this particular gentleman, there were no health or mental issues as we'd observed in the initial cases, back when we first realized some of these events were connected. Before the discovery, or I should say, before the websites were known to the authorities, or anyone really, outside the first participants.*

Mr. Bronwyn: *Participants, Doctor? I'd hardly call cold-blooded murderers 'participants'.*

Dr. Matthews: *Whatever you call them, Congressman, this man was different, at least from my past experience.*

Mr. Bronwyn: *Go on.*

Dr. Matthews: *I began to look at external factors outside the realm of the physical and psychological. To see if there was another —*

Mr. Bronwyn: *I'm not following, Doctor. What factors could be affecting these people besides the physical and emotional?*

Dr. Matthews: *I said outside the physical and psychological, not emotional.*

Mr. Bronwyn: *Excuse me?*

Dr. Matthews: *Congressman, if you'd let me finish, I think I can answer all of your questions.*

Mr. Bronwyn: *Just as long as you understand I'm the one asking them.*

*(laughter)*

Dr. Matthews: *Yes sir, of course.*

Mr. Bronwyn: *Proceed, Doctor.*

Dr. Matthews: *Thank you. And actually, before I go any further, I'd also like to thank my attorney.*

At this point, eyewitness testimony differs slightly. Some said that it was then that Dr. Matthews removed the pen from his breast pocket, and others said it was later, just before the assault, but no one diverged from the main point; it was an exceptionally quick and brutal attack.

Matthews' attorney, T. Richard Williams, Esq., turned toward his client and smiled awkwardly, apparently taken by surprise, as was everyone else, that he would be thanked in that way.

Dr. Matthews: *I mean it, Rich. Thank you.*

Mr. Williams: *Uh, you're welcome.*

(scattered laughter)

At this point, Dr. Matthews turned back to the committee as if the interruption had been the most natural interlude in the world, and resumed his testimony.

Dr. Matthews: *This person, whom I will refer to as TOWY P2, was not at all —*

Mr. Bronwyn: *P2? What does that mean?*

Dr. Matthews: *Phase two.*

Mr. Bronwyn: *I've never heard of any phase two.*

Dr. Matthews: *It's something I haven't disclosed, dealing with subjects outside the current study group.*

Mr. Bronwyn: *Why would you feel the need to change the criteria?*

Dr. Matthews: *That's what I'm trying to explain.*

Mr. Bronwyn: *No, Doctor, I think you're dancing around the issue, here. You've pretty much done a one-eighty on these protocols, protocols you helped develop, and I'd like to know why.*

Dr. Matthews: *Oh, dear. I can see that I'm just going to have to cut to the chase.*

Mr. Bronwyn: *I think you'd better cut to something.*

(laughter)

Ms. Ross-Levy: *Dr. Matthews, please just answer the questions.*

Mr. Bronwyn: *Thank you, Madam Chairman.*

Dr. Matthews: *Certainly, Madam Chairman.*

From eyewitness accounts: *It was at this point that Dr. Matthews sighed heavily and either picked up his pen from the table or removed it from his breast pocket, turned to his lawyer, and plunged it into the attorney's neck, puncturing the carotid artery, sending a fountain of blood spraying toward the members of the subcommittee and the C-SPAN2 witness camera, the live coverage immediately cut.*

*It wasn't known whether the chairman of the committee was hit in the face by the stream of blood as so many tasteless Internet rumors insisted, but she did faint and was treated for a concussion as a result of her fall during the subsequent chaos.*

Once Dr. Matthews was certain the man who'd been secretly fucking his wife was beyond saving, he stopped fighting the Capitol police officers that were trying to drag him off his lawyer and broke away, reaching inside his jacket as if searching for another weapon. The officers responded exactly as he'd hoped and opened fire, killing him instantly and relieving the psychological, but not emotional, pain from which he'd been suffering. Dr. Matthews had always prided himself on his lack of emotion, something that would indirectly lead to his death.

Had Congressman Bronwyn (R-FL) not been quite so impatient in his questioning, the doctor might have imparted some very valuable information on exactly why he considered psychological and emotional pain to be different, and why he'd joined the Towys but diverged (some would say perverted) from their original raison d'être, just as the man he referred to as TOWY P2 had done, a man whose son had suffered at the hands of a West Covina, California street gang.

Ironically, the person who best understood the doctor's motivations at that moment, T. Richard Williams, Esq., died on the floor of room 2141 of the Rayburn House Office Building less than two minutes and ten feet away from the man he'd cuckolded. He was a man definitely in closer contact with his emotions, which was why the good doctor's wife had turned to him for succor in the first place.

Rich Williams also immediately understood his client's testimony in a way that others would not for some time; namely, two years after the Pioneer, the TOWY movement had definitely taken a much more sinister turn from its arguably noble birth.

# Chapter Nineteen

**NSA Data Center – Outside Bluffdale, Utah**

"Freddie!"

Fred Dean's head popped up out of his cubicle like a gopher. Some of his co-workers had taken to calling him Flower behind his back, which was one of the stars of Meerkat Manor, a popular animal reality show that had been on the air a few years back.

Being that Flower was apparently a female meerkat that had been pushed around and eventually died during the course of the program, Freddie was none too pleased when he found out about it.

He mostly watched porn and illegally downloaded spy movies and surfed the Internet in his spare time, but had he seen the animal, which had black markings around it's eyes, it could have resembled someone who stayed up all night, as he usually did. He might have understood the humor, and even appreciated it, except for the barely concealed disdain beneath it. Freddie was a funny guy once you got to know him.

However, he wasn't feeling particularly appreciated at that moment.

Freddie rushed into this new supervisor's office, his third in the last six months, and closed the door behind him before being reminded to do so.

"What is this goddamn memo about?"

Freddie blinked. He knew he was about to get chewed out again, and he braced himself for the inevitable.

"I think I can find patient zero."

Like Freddie's previous eye-rolling supervisor and most of his co-workers, this one had had an immediate dislike of him, and had never attempted to hide it.

"I got that," the man sighed. "Look, Freddie, you know the heat we've been taking for things like this, don't you?"

"Yes sir, but – "

"You understand English, right? I mean, it is your first language, isn't it?"

"Yes, sir."

"I told you to end it."

"I was just requesting an extension. Sixty days."

"No."

"Thirty?"

His supervisor looked like he wanted to reach across the desk and throttle him, which wasn't that far from the truth.

"Who approved this, initially?"

"It was – "

"Never mind!" the supervisor said quickly. "I don't want to know. Just end it. I'm pulling your authorization. Effective immediately."

"Yes, sir," Freddie said glumly.

"Now get out."

Freddie left his office and went back to his cubicle. He hated this job. Nobody had any respect for his work.

He'd show them. He'd find the fucker on his own, and when the shit went down, he'd make sure to grab the credit.

***

Thane picked up his rental car at LAX and drove straight to the convalescent hospital in Compton. It was just about the most depressing place he'd ever seen, which was saying a lot for a police detective.

He'd been shocked as hell to get the call from the kid who claimed to work for the NSA, something that he hadn't been able to verify, and wasn't sure he wanted to. Thane had had his fill of the Feds with the task force, and certainly didn't want to be associated with some domestic spying bullshit. But the guy, who sounded like he was sixteen and insisted on being referred to as Mister Flowers, had only given him good information thus far, so he'd gotten the Captain to spring for his ticket.

The whole TOWY thing had gotten out of hand pretty quickly, and even though he sensed the Captain was still out to get him, if he came up with something big Thane was sure he'd forget all about the old beef as long as he could claim a hefty share of the credit.

He went to the nurses' station, where a bored product of the inner city's dearth of quality grocery stores led him to a room with peeling paint and four quads, all in various stages of what he imagined was a slow and painful descent into death or madness, or probably both.

He stopped her at the door, and motioned for the nurse to step back into the hall out of earshot of the guy he'd come to see.

"Just how aware is this guy?" Thane asked. "Does he know what the hell is going on around him?"

Nurse Ratched looked at him for a moment and popped her gum.

"He can hear. Sometimes he'll squeeze a hunk a sheet when I say something. Blink at me. Course he might be takin' a shit in his pants, too. I just call the orderly for that. 'Bout it."

"Will he understand what I say?"

"Couldn't tell you. But he don't react much." She laughed and told Thane a story about an earthquake that knocked all three of his roommates out of bed. All this guy did was 'squeeze a hunk a sheet' and stare at an aerobics show on the TV. "Probably starin' at that ass, know what I'm sayin'?"

Thane nodded ruefully and walked back in the room. He went over to the third bed and checked the name on the chart.

*Phillip Maxwell Cody.* Known to friends and foes alike as Big Max.

The living skeleton in the bed didn't look much like he was ever very big, let alone possessed a criminal record as long as three arms, but Thane supposed a lot had changed for the son of a bitch since the accident.

From what he knew about the guy, Thane wasn't at all sympathetic.

***

Anita didn't stand up when the Captain walked in, nor would he have expected her to. There was no more informality between them; now it was all business.

"We got a warrant for his apartment, computer, all of it. I want you to take Manish over there."

"Who's Manish?" Anita asked. She didn't like the idea of snooping around Thane's apartment while the Captain had him out of town on some wild goose chase.

"New kid. I can't pronounce his last name. IT guy. He'll put a little...hell, I don't know what it is. Something on his computer. So you can watch what he does. Keystroke something-or-other."

"Is this really necessary?"

The Captain leaned across his desk. "You haven't exactly gotten me anything I can use," he said sarcastically. "So yeah, it's necessary." He pulled a file from his inbox and leaned back to shuffle through it, ignoring her. Anita considered waiting him out, but instead she got up to leave.

At the door, she had an impulse, and turned to face him.

"Got a copy of the warrant?" she asked.

He looked up and she saw it in his eyes. No need to hang around for his bullshit. There wasn't any warrant. Whatever he held against Thane, Captain Myers wasn't about to let it go. He was determined to bring him down, no matter what.

"What was that?" he asked.

"Nothing."

As she opened the door to leave, Anita heard him mumble something about getting her a copy as soon as he could, but she'd already gotten everything she needed.

***

On the flight back, Thane kept thinking about Big Max Cody. For a quadriplegic who'd barely communicated with the outside world since he'd emerged from his coma, he'd displayed a helluva reaction to that picture of Melissa Williamson. And his eyes lit up like a Christmas tree when he showed him the fax of her bloody tattoo. Not like *he'd* killed her, but more like she'd tried to kill *him*.

He wouldn't swear to it, but the son of a bitch had seemed scared.

Thane wondered if Max knew what the tattoo meant, given the fact he'd done a few months in the Coast Guard back in the day before getting kicked out for dealing smack. *Probably wasn't sharp enough to learn Morse Code.* Thane suspected what would have scared him more was the arrangement of those dots and dashes, anyway, and the crude picture they formed.

Twin graves.

*Take one with you.*

Maybe there was something to Mister Flowers' theory, after all. He'd have to call him again when he landed and brace him a little under the guise of an update on Big Max. Try and get some more background on who really came up with that tat. He didn't figure it was Melissa. Pretty ingenious, actually.

Flowers liked to talk, and Thane was an expert at getting information from people who don't know they're giving it up, but this guy was smart. He insisted on relaying most information by untraceable cell phone, committing nothing too incriminating to emails, and insisting Thane do the same. It was annoying as hell, but effective. But Thane sensed he was just a little too smart for his own good.

*If you really work for the NSA, nothing's untraceable, dumbass.*

Thane laughed at the thought of some pimple-faced, overly chatty junior analyst being surprised at his workstation with an arrest warrant and a set of handcuffs, which was how he imagined Flowers ending up if he actually did work for the intelligence service.

Thane ordered another Budweiser from the flight attendant and opened his notebook, going over the list of names he'd gotten from Flowers, some of which were pretty colorful. Jesus Two Bears and El Culo de Arica, in particular, would make for some pretty interesting reading if everything turned out to be true and someone wanted to write a book about it, which he suspected was Flowers' true motivation.

The names he was most interested in at that moment were the two locals, Charlie Sanderson and Sarah Crane.

\*\*\*

Charlie couldn't bear to go back home, so after he left Sarah's place, he'd checked into a cheap motel near the airport. He figured he'd stay there until his money ran out and then think of what to do.

Right now, thinking was not on the agenda.

He watched TV constantly, leaving it on the cable news stations until it was time for the local news, at which point he'd switch over, waiting for stories about more TOWY deaths, which were now coming more frequently.

He watched in horror as footage of a near riot at a local cemetery was played over and over, until he finally shut off the TV for the first time in days.

A man who worked for a local florist had apparently pulled up in front of his ex-wife's apartment building with a van full of fresh cut wedding arrangements, left the motor running, and gone inside to slash the throat of his children's mother before cutting his own wrists and collapsing on top of her.

They remained in that position until their son and daughter came home from school and found their parents stacked up like bloody cordwood.

The couple had been arguing over visitation schedules still lingering from a recent divorce, and even though none of that had anything to do with the website, apparently some neighborhood kids had spray painted the TOWY symbol on the sidewalk in front of the building after the fact.

At first it seemed like just a random event that vandals had corrupted, and Charlie was absurdly relieved by that fact. A few hours later, however, it was discovered that the man had indeed frequented the TOWY website, and even gone into a local tattoo parlor looking to get the TOWY symbol inscribed onto his arm. When the shop owner asked him about it, the man became upset and left. Tattoo artists in the area had been asked to voluntarily report any requests for the symbol, as mandatory reporting had already been nixed after the local chapter of the ACLU threatened a lawsuit.

The results of the police entreaties were mixed.

Some were cooperating, others were advertising. There were even rather tasteless "two-for-one" coupons floating around on underground sites and alternative weeklies.

It really became a circus when the florist's family showed up to bury him on the same day at the same cemetery as his late ex-wife, which was just a little too much for her brothers. The resulting melee made national news, and was just more publicity for the whole TOWY phenomenon.

The next day there were rumors that two founders of TOWY, supposedly a guy and a girl, were going to show up at a local mall, and several idiotic teenagers showed up and got into a gun battle with local police.

All of this was being watched closely but separately by Charlie and Sarah. Neither one wanted to be apart from the other, but neither one quite knew how to heal the rift that now existed between them.

Most young lovers were tested by petty jealousies and childish misunderstandings; silly texts or whispered gossip. Charlie and Sarah had to figure out how to bridge issues of literal life and death, and it was something neither of them was able to figure out.

Ironically, in the end it was Brad who brought them back together.

***

"I found the girl."

Brad nearly dropped the phone. "Thank fuck."

"She and that stepson of yours kinda dropped off the face of the earth while ago, but she's got an apartment not far from you. Not sure about him, yet."

Brad frowned. "You mean they're not together?"

"Not that I can tell."

"I need them both."

"I'll let you know, then."

Brad hung up the phone after getting the rest of the information that had been obtained. This guy was nowhere near as professional as the man in the windbreaker, but he would have to do. He could still use her to get to him. Maybe this way would even work out better.

*One at a time might make things easier.*

He picked up the phone and called Sarah.

***

As much as she hated to admit it, what she'd found on Thane's computer deeply troubled Anita. He hadn't been sharing a lot of information with the task force, and he appeared to know quite a bit about some murders that seemed clearly to be TOWY related, possibly even the initial crimes. But it was all so confusing. The email address of the person with whom he was secretly communicating was untraceable. Even Manish the IT guy couldn't track it back to the source.

Anita was careful not to share too much with him since she knew it would get back to Myers, but just the headers and the email address of the shadowy source Thane had been exchanging information with, somebody called Flowers, had set off alarm bells.

"Whoever's sending those emails is up to something," Manish told her. "No one has that level of security outside the NSA."

*What the fuck is Thane doing?*

"It's pretty impressive, actually," Manish continued on the phone. "Let me know when you have more."

*Yeah, right.* "Will do, thanks," Anita said, and hung up before Manish could ask her any more questions. She figured she had at least a week or so before the kid realized what side of the bread his butter was on and started voluntarily filling in Myers behind her back. The Captain wouldn't want to be so obvious as to immediately tell the kid to spy on his superior, but he'd get to that eventually if she didn't find something pretty quickly.

Thane had been swamped since he started working the task force, and they hadn't been together since their amazing sexual marathon, but Anita was eager to talk to him about his trip to

California. He'd been just a little too casual about the trip and she sensed it had something to do with this TOWY thing.

One of the emails she'd gotten off his computer referred to someone or something named Clairebear, and there was a number attached that looked like it might be a case number or incident report, something official that she hadn't yet figured out.

Thane wasn't trusting too much to his keyboard; he was probably using a drop phone, which made her even more suspicious.

Why would a detective use a drop phone?

\*\*\*

Thane found Brad's name and address through his search for Charlie, which had been surprisingly fruitless. This Sarah sounded more promising, actually. She had an arrest record almost as long as Big Max, but no convictions. Her dad had been that senator who'd died in a car accident one state over. *Probably got her out of a few,* Thane thought. He didn't care about that, though. He'd do the same for his own kid, if he had to. Sarah's mother was a rich bitch who'd taken up with her ex-husband's chief of staff before the body was cold. *Nice.* Thane didn't even have to source that one; it had been in the fucking newspaper.

Sarah seemed more like the type to go a little wild. Charlie had nothing, no record of any kind. Seemed like a nice, quiet kid. Dead parents, though. Life's tough.

But when he checked out his stepfather, Brad, a whole list of shady dealings popped up going back at least fifteen years. No convictions, but from what Thane could tell, the guy was a scumbag. Lots of civil suits, lots of people who felt ripped off but couldn't prove it. A real douchebag.

*Now that's the type of guy who could use one of those Towys on his ass.*

# **Chapter Twenty**

Thane sensed something was bothering Anita, but he'd been too goddamn busy to talk to her. The day he got back from California somebody called in a tip that two TOWY founders were on their way to Willow Creek Mall to turn themselves in, and then someone, probably the same asshole, had put out the same information on the Internet.

That was when Thane decided to take matters into his own hands.

***

"Who?" Sarah asked.

"Brad. Charlie's stepdad."

Sarah's blood ran cold. "What do you want?" she asked. "How did you get this number?"

Brad ignored the second question, a fact Sarah noticed immediately.

"Haven't seen Charlie lately," Brad said. "I'm kind of worried."

*I'll bet you are.* "I haven't seen him," she said coldly.

"Do you know where he is?"

"No, I don't."

"Well, maybe you could stop by and pick up a few of his things. Give them to him the next time you see him."

"Why would I do that?"

"I'm going to be leaving tonight," Brad said. "Not sure when I'm coming back. They belonged to his mother."

Sarah stopped breathing for a moment. She knew Charlie would want whatever had belonged to his mom.

"What is it?" she asked.

"Odds and ends. But there's a letter. It's sealed, addressed to Charlie. I know he'd want it."

Sarah's mind raced. "Why don't you just leave it all on the porch and I'll pick it up tomorrow?"

There was a pause.

"I can do that. I'll put it out tonight. Before I leave. In case you change your mind."

"Good."

"You won't even have to see me."

Sarah hung up before he could say anything else. Brad was probably lying, but what if he wasn't?

*Fuck.*

She had to call Charlie.

***

Brad hung up the phone and threw some random junk into a cardboard box, dragging it out onto the porch. He preferred to get both of them over tonight, but whatever. Whether one or both showed up would be fine. One of them would lead to the other. He was quite sure of that.

He turned off all the lights and sat down at his desk, where the window faced the front of the house. He took out the .38, checked the cylinder, and locked it back into place, settling in for the long haul. After a few minutes staring out the window, he grabbed a few more flat points and put them in his shirt pocket.

He'd be ready no matter who showed up.

***

Anita hung up, fuming. All the late night calls and sexy texts and Thane was acting like they were casual acquaintances or something.

*'I've got shit to do?' 'I've got shit to do?' Why is he acting like that?*

After a moment, she understood. Thane knew how to push her buttons. Unlike her husband, Thane could always get the reaction he wanted from her.

*That's why I love him.*

Anita stopped and thought about that for a minute, and realized it was true. She was in love with Thane.

*So was he trying to make me mad? Or was it real?*

She went back to her computer and went through the files she had on Thane.

Turned out, it didn't really make a difference.

*** 

Thane hung up and studied the text on his drop phone. It was just four numbers. They'd spoken on the phone after his trip to LA, and that was when Flowers informed him that someone in his department had been monitoring their communications. Flowers was very different on that call, so serious that Thane believed him. He figured it was probably Myers.

*No wonder the asshole paid for my trip.*

"I'll text you with the info when I get it," Flowers had said. "Radio silence until you hear back."

*Yeah, right. Radio silence. Kid sounds like he's playing detective.*

But the text really knocked the wind out of him. As soon as he received it, Thane angrily dialed Flowers. The number had already been disconnected.

Thane stared at the text. Four numbers. Anita's badge number.

"Goddamnit!" he screamed, and threw his phone against the wall.

*He's using her against me.*

But was that really true? Or was she a willing participant?

Suddenly their time together seemed like a goddamn lie. She was just another ball-busting bitch like his ex and her attorney. Everybody piling on to get a piece of the pie.

Thane was as pissed off as he'd ever been in his life. At least his ex had a reason for acting the way she did. He didn't like it, but their years together weren't always pretty; plenty of blame to go around, there. But Anita? What reason did she have to betray him like that?

The more he thought about it, the sicker he felt. Usually he could just shake it off and be done with it. He'd left more people behind than he cared to admit.

This was different. He loved this one.

And that was what made it sting.  He left the house in a rage, ready to kick some ass.

***

When she called, Charlie was in the shower, his first of the week. Even his shock and grief was not enough to keep Charlie comfortable with his own rank smell after being cooped up so long in the tiny motel room. What maid service there was, he had consistently refused for fear of being seen by someone who might report the presence of a teenager at the motel, which might bring him unwanted attention.

He'd gotten out of the shower and was immediately engrossed in the coverage of the local mall shootout, which was covered wall-to-wall on both local and national news outlets. Of particular interest to Charlie was the detective in charge of the task force, who almost seemed as if he knew who they were. Like he was subtly sending a message to him and Sarah. He wondered if he should call her.

He watched the coverage for almost an hour more before he realized he'd gotten a voicemail.

He looked at the caller ID.

Sarah.

*"Hi Charlie...it's me. Listen, Brad's leaving town tomorrow. He's got some of your mom's stuff. He's going to leave it out on the porch. Tomorrow. He's leaving it out tomorrow. I don't think you should go over there, so I'll go over tomorrow. Since it won't be out there tonight. I'll call when I have it."* There was a long pause. *"I love you, Charlie."*

Charlie called her back but she didn't pick up. Had she seen the mall shooting? Maybe she was upset. Maybe she still wasn't ready to talk. He listened to the message several more times before he realized what she was doing. He checked out of the motel, determined to end it all.

***

Anita stared at the computer screen. There it was. She grabbed her phone and called Thane. Voicemail.

*Where the fuck are you?*

She went back to the files and tried to figure out what his next move would be.

***

Thane grabbed him by the collar. "I got your number, goof."

The "goof" gave a mighty shove and Thane practically flew backwards, stumbling against a table, nearly falling over chairs. A big guy from the kitchen was now standing in the doorway, but the bartender waved him off. Someone touched Thane's shoulder and he turned in anger, but he immediately softened when he saw who it was.

"Jesus, Cookie," he slurred. It was his favorite waitress, the one whose real name, once again, eluded him. "For a minute I thought you were Goodbody."

"Who?" She smiled and shook her head, looking at him with a mixture of concern and pity that made him feel even worse, and he realized he needed to get the hell out of there. He patted her hand and nodded towards the bartender, but he was already taking other drink orders.

"Nobody gives a shit what I do," he mumbled.

"I do."

Thane turned to see Anita standing there.

***

Charlie took the bus to Brad's, which meant he'd still have a hike to get there from the nearest bus stop. He hoped he'd be in time.

***

"I know it's not you."

Thane blinked and tried to focus on what she was saying. "Not me, what?"

"The Towys," Anita answered. "I know it's not you."

Thane threw her hand off his shoulder. "What the fuck are you talking about?"

"I thought maybe...you were involved...not involved, I mean not doing it, or anything. Maybe just..." Her voice trailed off. She clearly didn't know how to tell him that she had thought he might actually have been working directly with the creators of the website.

"Involved?"

"No! I don't think that, now," she pleaded. "Just maybe that you know more than you're telling the feds."

"Like what?"

Two people exited the restaurant, bundling themselves up against the cool night air. Anita tried to steer Thane farther away from the door, but he shrugged her off again.

"Like who's behind that website."

Thane sneered and walked towards his car. "I know lots of shit."

"Wait a minute," she said, and walked ahead of him.

He stopped and glared at her. "You know lots of shit, too, don't you?"

"What's that supposed to mean?"

"You know goddamn well what it means, Sherlock."

He brushed past her and she followed him. "Okay, I'm sorry. I got roped in. But what would you expect me to do?"

Thane whirled around. "How about a little honesty?"

Anita stopped in her tracks. It stung, and they both knew it. He had never lied to her; maybe he'd been slow to report what he'd found to the feds, but he'd never lied to her. He'd just been doing his job. She could not say the same.

Thane stood there looking at her, slightly unsteady, waiting for her to respond, but there was nothing she could say. For the first time she saw real hurt in his eyes, and that made her feel even worse. He loved her, she knew that now, and she also knew that she'd blown it. He was not an easy man to love, but when he did, he put it all out there. Trust was something he valued above all else, and that trust had been shattered.

"Nothing to say, huh?"

She could barely meet his eyes, and after a moment, he turned to get into his car. Had he not been just a little drunk, or had she been able to stifle the impulse to reach out for him, both Thane and Anita might have lived to see the morning.

***

Sarah called her mother before she left. She wasn't sure why she needed to do that, but somehow it felt right. She was very happy to hear from her daughter, and the two of them cried a bit before ending the call, which was very brief. She made Sarah promise to come home for a visit the following day.

She never saw her daughter again.

\*\*\*

Anita reached for Thane. She had more to confess, more truth to tell, but what she really wanted was to touch him. She needed to touch, feel him, connect with him, if only for an instant.

Thane felt her hand on his shoulder. He, too, longed for her touch. Longed to connect. But because he was drunk, he was unsteady. And because he was hurt, he was angry.

He turned awkwardly and lost his balance on the curb, flailing his powerful arms just as she moved closer. Anita fell to the sidewalk, blood gushing from her nose, the two of them connecting physically in a way neither had intended. She looked up at him in shock, not because she thought it had been on purpose, but because she had come close to blacking out.

It was more confusion than accusation, but all Thane saw was the look in her eye and the blood on her face. He was immediately filled with such shame and revulsion at what he'd done that he was in his car and driving away before she could say a word.

\*\*\*

Brad bolted upright, nearly spilling his scotch. He peered out the window, pocketed the gun, and left through the back door.

\*\*\*

Anita ran to her car, wiping her face with her sleeve. She thought she knew where Thane was going; it had been in his notes. The notes she had found on his computer. The notes she wished she'd never seen. In his condition, she didn't trust his judgment and felt responsible for what might happen. He was impulsive and angry, and she'd seen what he was capable of doing in that state of mind.

She checked her notebook for the address and sped into the night.

***

Anita was right about Thane's intentions. She was right about his anger. She was right about his first impulse after that argument. He wanted to heal the rift between them as badly as she did, and the way to do that was to end it that very night. Thane was on his way to the address she had copied into her notebook from his computer.

Ironically, the one thing Anita had not factored into her decision was the one thing that changed his own. The one thing that made her happiest about their terrible fight. The one bright spot of the evening, borne of their awful confrontation.

Anita knew that Thane loved her. It was why he was so devastated at her betrayal.

It was what drove them both, and why their final missed connection would have such tragic consequences.

Thane turned back around and went to find Anita.

***

Sarah raced towards Brad's house, hoping against hope that Charlie had gotten her message.

***

Brad was barely a quarter block away when he saw her striding towards his front door. He froze, unsure what to do. It seemed like her knock echoed throughout the quiet neighborhood. He stepped behind his neighbor's oak and watched her turn and walk away. He thought he'd missed his chance, but then she stopped in the driveway and peered inside the garage window.

*Good thing I parked down the street.*

But he was late. His plan was to make it appear as if he wasn't home, so that if Sarah showed up for the box of junk, he could drag her in the house quickly. It looked as if everything had gone perfectly, except he'd forgotten about the car until it was too late, having to now stalk his prey from outside.

*Goddamnit.*

But then the stupid bitch went back to the porch and knocked again. She barely even looked at the box, which he thought was strange, but it was enough time for him to run up the walk and hit her with the gun.

She fell forward, stunned, but she wasn't unconscious. Not at all like it happened in the movies. Brad opened the door and practically threw her inside, immediately binding her hands. Good thing he hadn't just stuck the gun in her back. She was a lot heavier than he thought she'd be. Could have put up a hell of a fight.

Brad was in such a hurry and the porch was so dark that he never noticed the gun now resting just outside his front door, like an ominous welcome mat.

***

Charlie walked towards the house, tired but purposeful. He didn't see Sarah's car, out front, which he considered a good sign.

***

Anita's husband nearly had a heart attack when he opened the door and Thane was standing there, but the stunned man let him in and even allowed him to search the house. Once Thane was sure he wasn't lying, he left without saying another word, leaving him speechless.

***

Brad stared at Anita, who was now tied to a chair at his kitchen table with a gag in her mouth. She looked really angry and really bloody. The back of her head seemed fine, but her nose was like a faucet, for some reason. When he'd tried to wipe it with a paper towel, she lunged at him like a crazy person, and so he'd tied her up.

*How is this not Sarah? Who the fuck is she?*

"Do you know Charlie?" he asked, and though she couldn't speak, he saw in her eyes that she recognized the name. "What about Sarah?"

Anita just looked at him. Charlie and Sarah were the two names in Thane's computer she figured were his top suspects, and this asshole was the one she thought he'd come to see first.

Too bad she'd been only half right.

Brad could tell she knew them both by the way she reacted. He decided it would be better if he just looked for her ID instead of taking out the gag and asking her, but she looked as mean and angry as anyone he'd ever seen.

He'd have to be careful.

\*\*\*

Charlie walked around to the side of the house. Most of the lights were off, so he didn't know if Brad was home or not, but he wasn't taking any chances. He went to the shed, grabbed an axe, and made his way to the breaker box by the light of the Hunter's moon.

\*\*\*

Brad managed to remove Anita's wallet, but just as he flipped it open, the kitchen light went off, throwing them into an eerie gray darkness. He nearly fainted when he looked down and saw the glint of her badge.

What woke him from his stupor was the sound of the back door creaking open, which meant only one thing. Grateful he'd left it unlocked, he moved behind Anita and pointed his gun towards the kitchen doorway.

\*\*\*

As Charlie was sneaking in the back door, Sarah was rifling through the cardboard box on the front porch. There was no envelope, which was what she was most interested in, but at least Charlie hadn't been here. She stood up and was about to shut off her phone light when the beam found Anita's .38 special a couple of feet away.

"What the fuck?" she said to herself, but before the words were completely spoken, she heard a gunshot from inside the house. "Charlie!" she screamed, and picked up the gun.

\*\*\*

Charlie was sneaking towards the kitchen when the shot rang out. He instinctively dropped to the floor and probably would have remained there but for the sound of his name being called from the front of the darkened house.

\*\*\*

Thane pulled up just as the second shot was fired. He leapt out of his car and ran up the driveway to the door with his weapon drawn, peering into the darkness.

"Police!"

Anita, who had caused the first shot when she lunged at Brad, fell to the floor and was unable to prevent him from shooting Charlie with the second round as he ran through the kitchen towards the sound of Sarah's voice.

She was, however, able to slip free of her ties and tackle Brad. As they struggled on the floor of the kitchen, another shot rang out, and Anita rolled off.

Sarah entered, saw Charlie on the floor, and pointed her gun at Brad, who had dropped his weapon. He rose to his feet and raised his hands.

"Don't shoot," he said.

Sarah licked her lips and tried to pull the trigger, but Thane pushed her aside and shot Brad, who dropped like a stone.

Sarah ran to Charlie and Thane ran to Anita, but there was no hope for either of them. Thane collected the guns and walked over to Sarah, who was whispering something over and over in Charlie's ear. It sounded to Thane like 'fuck you chickless', but he couldn't be sure.

He knelt beside them and checked Charlie's pulse, just as he had done for Anita, with the same result. Whatever words left unsaid between them would remain forever so, and now Thane was running on pure instinct.

As the sound of sirens rose in the distance, Thane finally tore Sarah from Charlie's body and put his keys in her hand.

"My car's out front. Take it around back, in the alley. Wait for me there."

"What?" Sarah mumbled, confused.

Thane took her face in his hands and forced her to focus. "I know about you and Charlie," he said. "Leave the motor running. We have a lot to talk about. Go!"

She nodded dumbly and started to leave when there was a moan behind them. Brad was sitting up, leaning against the refrigerator.

Thane raised his gun to finish him off, but this time it was Sarah who pushed him aside, wrenching the gun from his hand in a rage. Before Thane could stop her, she put the muzzle against Brad's forehead and pulled the trigger.

She turned around and held out the weapon, her blood spattered face shining eerily in the moonlight streaming through the windows.

He took the gun from her and she walked towards the front of the house without another word.

Thane leaned down and kissed Anita, whose lips were still soft and warm.

He stood up and started to tell her how much he loved her, but the sirens, which were now very loud, pulled him from his reverie.

Thane began to leave through the back door, but as he turned for one last look at the grisly scene, he had a thought and walked towards the front of the house, looking for the interior door to the garage.

***

Thane sprinted through the back yard, which was almost a quarter acre, and easily hopped the chain link fence at the rear of the property as the house burst into flames behind him.

Sarah was there, just as he knew she would be, and they drove away in silence as police responders waited out front for the fire department to arrive, guns drawn.

**Most Pirated Album of the Year**

# <u>EPILOGUE</u>

Freddie Flowers, the nom-de guerre of the literary sensation behind the New York Times bestseller detailing the inside story of the TOWY phenomenon, waited patiently at each book signing, eager to talk to his fans and reveling in their adulation. He loved to talk and the buyers of the book never tired of listening, unlike some people he could name at his previous job.

At a bookstore in Santa Barbara, not all that far from one of the earliest and most notorious murder-suicides, he had just finished chatting amiably with some of the last stragglers in line and was beginning to pack up when a father and daughter appeared and plopped down an open book, the final passage highlighted.

*No one knows where Sarah ended up and Detective Parks hasn't spoken a word on the subject since the Grand Jury cleared him to return to work. It has been theorized that Sarah, like so many of her followers, left this mortal coil and 'took one with her', as they say. Suicide might seem to many a fitting ending to the strange saga of the grizzled cop and the naïve criminal who crossed paths at such an intimate yet explosive moment of their lives; the perfect coda to the global phenomenon called TOWY.*

*I, for one, hope not. Were I ever to speak to Sarah, I would tell her where she went wrong, and perhaps advise how she might actually accomplish the original goal; to clean up the filth of society and allow the rest of us to breathe easier for having known the Towys were out there somewhere, acting as judge, jury, and executioner.*

*I might even have some advice on how to use a guy like Detective Parks.*

The man formerly known as Fred Dean looked up. Thane and Sarah weren't smiling, but neither did they appear threatening.

"We've got a lot to talk about," Thane said.

Sarah nodded. "Lots."

www.OakAnderson.com

# About the Author

Oak Anderson is an author, artist, and marketing strategist. His imagination has taken him to places he couldn't help but note down, eventually crafting his ideas into a thought provoking story. After stealing minutes here and there over the last few years, he eventually completed his first fiction novel, Take One With You.

CPSIA information can be obtained
at www.ICGtesting.com
Printed in the USA
LVOW11s1806300117

522613LV00002B/524/P